The face of death

I heard Flip say, "Shoes . . . a pair of shoes." He was standing still, ankle-deep in the leaves. Before I caught up with him, he'd whirled around facing me. "Behind me," he said in a funny, tight voice. I couldn't figure out what had come over him. "Come on," he said, "we're getting out of here." But he didn't move. And neither did I.

He was swallowing air fast and breathing, "Jesus, oh Jesus." I looked past him and saw a pair of shoes sticking up out of the leaves at a funny, splayfooted angle. They were leaf-colored and round-toed like old construction boots. They didn't make any sense to me. I kept staring while Flip kind of half turned and tried to get another look out of the corner of his eye. Underneath the leaves, past the shoes, I saw what looked like a pile of old clothes. And farther up something else, something shiny.

There was a breeze that whisked the leaves around a little. I was staring at the shiny place, and then right away, I was looking at a grin. A big, yawning grin right down on ground level and a black eye socket. A leaf was over the other one. And some hair on the clean, white bone of a skull's forehead . . .

DREAMLAND
LAKE

DREAMLAND
LAKE

RICHARD PECK

PUFFIN BOOKS

The verse on page 67 is entitled
"Frankenstein by Mary W. Shelley"
from SHRINKLETS by Maurice Sagoff.
Copyright © 1970 by Maurice Sagoff.
Reprinted by permission of Doubleday
& Company, Inc.

The poem on pages 131–132 is entitled
"The High School Band." Reprinted with
permission of The Macmillan Company from
THE SELF-MADE MAN AND OTHER POEMS
by Reed Whittemore. © Reed Whittemore 1959.

PUFFIN BOOKS
Published by the Penguin Group
Penguin Putnam Books for Young Readers,
345 Hudson Street, New York, New York 10014, U.S.A.
Penguin Books Ltd, 27 Wrights Lane, London W8 5TZ, England
Penguin Books Australia Ltd, Ringwood, Victoria, Australia
Penguin Books Canada Ltd, 10 Alcorn Avenue, Toronto, Ontario, Canada M4V 3B2
Penguin Books (N.Z.) Ltd, 182-190 Wairau Road, Auckland 10, New Zealand

Penguin Books Ltd, Registered Offices: Harmondsworth, Middlesex, England

First published in the United States of America by Holt, Rinehart, Winston, 1973
Published by Puffin Books,
a division of Penguin Putnam Books for Young Readers, 2000

10 9 8 7 6 5 4 3 2 1

LIBRARY OF CONGRESS CATALOGING-IN-PUBLICATION DATA
Peck, Richard, date
Dreamland Lake / Richard Peck.
    p. cm.
Summary: Best friends since grade school, thirteen-year-old Flip and Brian
find that their friendship and their lives are forever changed after they
discover a dead man near Dreamland Lake.
ISBN 0-14-130812-5 (pbk.)
[1. Mystery and detective stories. 2. Friendship—Fiction.] I. Title.
PZ7.P338 Dr 2000 [Fic]—dc21 99-055400

Printed in the United States of America

For Mary Jane
and Curt Crotty

Spring

One

There was a dead man in the weeds up at the woodsy end of Dreamland Lake. He'd been there the better part of the winter, freezing and thawing like the lake. But, by the end of March, the trees were beginning to leaf out. The little creek that fed into the lake was almost at flood tide, which meant you had to take a running jump to clear it. The crocuses were up—purple and yellow—and the violets were on the way

If you had all morning, you could count every tree in it, so it isn't a real woods. Any more than Dreamland Lake is a real lake. Nowadays, people call it the duck pond. There isn't much you can do with it except feed the ducks. And nobody does that except the Park Department and a few little kids with bread crumbs who only come there in the summer.

Some of the old-timers around here, like Mrs. Garrison, still call the place Dreamland Park because they remember it from way back. The days when it was right out in the country. A mile from the city limits, with a streetcar track that had a turnaround at the gates. It was an amusement park in those days—with a dance palace the Baptists closed, and a race track the county closed, and a roller coaster that swooped right down level with the lake. The roller coaster had the quickest end of all. It caught fire one night in 1922 and burned right down to the water. But by then, there wasn't much amusement park left so the fire chief let it burn itself out.

Then later, the town grew out in that direction, took the land for back taxes, and turned it into a regular city park named Marquette Park. They cleaned it up, put in picnic tables, and turned the dance palace into a clubhouse for the tennis players. And they put mallards and teals and a pair of swans in Dreamland Lake. But they left the woods up at the end of it. And a half century after the roller coaster burned, that was where Flip and I found the dead man.

I'm writing all this down pretty much like it happened. If some of it sounds like a murder mystery or something, remember, it isn't. But that's the way Flip and I saw it at the time. Mainly because we wanted to, I guess. And partly because somebody else wanted us to. Nobody killed the dead man as far as I know. He probably didn't have an enemy in the world—or a friend, for that matter. We never thought about him as being alive, ever. It was the death angle that got to us.

We were on this local history kick. Flip hated English, but he loved looking things up. He was just going into his amateur photography phase, so books on How to Build Your Own Home Dark Room drew him to the Coolidge Middle School library. It was the first good library we had entrance to. The grade school one was mainly full of dog stories by Albert Payson Terhune. And we'd been barred from the public library downtown since the time we dropped the persimmons down the stairwell and they splattered all over the Reserved Books desk. That was in fifth grade, but librarians remember.

So Flip came across this book in the school library and got wrapped up in local history. Like I said, he went through these phases, and I used to go through most of them with him. I used to, a couple of years ago, when we were kind of a team. But that was a couple of years ago. We aren't a team anymore, and I guess that's why I'm telling this story.

He came racing up to the bike rack after school one day waving an old, dusty, brown book. It was *A Centennial History of the City of Dunthorpe, Black Hawk County, and Environs* by one Estella Winkler Bates.

"Can you believe it?" Flip said. "Somebody wrote a book just about this county. And look, nobody's checked it out since 1952. This is a real, undiscovered find!"

We hunkered down right there, with our backs against the bike rack, and started in to find out how Estella Winkler Bates had managed to fill three hundred and two pages with nothing but local history.

5

The title page said that the book was in commemoration of the one hundredth anniversary of the first settlement. They had this big celebration back in 1929 which inspired Estella Winkler Bates to sit down and write a Cultural and Economic History. Across from the first page was a photograph of the Centennial Pageant. It showed a lot of old-fashioned, flapper-looking girls wrapped in the American flag hanging onto an old, open Buick and holding up a big banner that said:

1829—1929 A CENTURY OF GREATNESS

After that, the going was uphill because the Bates style was heavy. It seems they held the celebration in the fall of 1929 because she started out,

In this season of mists and mellow fruitfulness, we point with particular pride to the pioneer perseverance that brought this metropolis of the plains and the verdure of its surrounding loam out of the rough lawlessness and the unbroken sod of its primeval period. We point, too, ahead to yet another century of promise and perpetual progress—we have come from the Conestoga Wagon to the modern automobile. From the Pony Express to the modern aeroplane and dirigible. From the. . . .

Flip stopped reading and said, "What's she talking about? We never had any Pony Express around here. That was way out in St. Joseph, Missouri."

"She's full of hot air," I told him. "All she likes is P's."

"What?" said Flip.

"P's," I said, and pointed them all out. "Look—

6

point, particular, pride, pioneer, perseverance, primeval, promise, perpetual, progress. She's in love with P's. Forget it. Take it back to the library before you lose it and have to pay for it."

"And dirigibles," Flip said. "She thought we were going to spend the next century flying around in dirigibles."

"Yeah," I said, "dirigibles. That's a laugh."

"I'll tell you another one," Flip said. "You don't even know what dirigibles are." That's the kind of challenge that used to end up with Flip and me trying to stomp one another's heads in. But we were in the seventh grade by then, and trying hard to leave that kind of childishness behind us.

"Dirigible is some old kind of airplane," I said.

"Wrong," Flip said. "I knew you didn't know. It's an air*ship*. A big bag full of hydrogen or helium with a little cabin underneath where people rode—called a gondola. I knew you didn't know it as soon as I read the word."

"That's what I meant," I replied, and tried to look wise.

"Well, you didn't," Flip said, and turned to the Table of Contents to see if the book might pick up any later on. There, about halfway through, was a chapter called "Dreamland Park: Dunthorpe's Own Coney Island."

"What's this?" Flip said.

"Hot air," I explained. "There's no such a place as a Dreamland Park around here. It's something like Estella Winkler Bates would think up when she was getting carried away."

"I guess I'll take this home and read it when I have some peace and quiet," Flip said. He closed the book and tossed it into his bike basket.

But that night, he called up and said Dreamland Park was not hot air, and that it had been an actual amusement park, and that its remains were no more than two blocks from the street we both lived on.

He quoted from Estella Winkler Bates for evidence:

> Dreamland Park, that popular and mildly notorious resort that flourished from the turn of the century until the Great War, lured the "shady ladies" and sporting gents of the period. Following an afternoon of harness racing, the crowds thronged to the commodious dance palace, the capacious veranda of which commanded a prospect of Dreamland Lake itself. Over this picturesque patch of moon-kissed water arched the delicate tracery of a cast-iron bridge, illuminated by the bewitching glimmer of Japanese lanterns.

"Knock it off," I said to Flip. "I can't take any more."

"Shut up and listen," he said.

> Providing a dramatic backdrop for this scene of melodious revelry was the giant roller coaster —a scenic railway which elevated its passengers to dizzying heights, only to plunge them, to the accompaniment of their own breathless screams, to the very surface of the lake itself.

"Are you going to read out the whole book?" I asked Flip.

"There's just a little bit more on the park," he said. "Listen."

Alas, the erosions of time and taste and an awesome conflagration which consumed the roller coaster spelled the end of the fantastic fun fair's palmy period. Today, it forms a part of the tranquil city park bearing the name of Pere Marquette, early explorer of our region and man of God. One hundred and eighty-one acres of Nature's Own Preserve mutes the purposeful roar of our expanding metropolis. Dreamland Park is now but a dream! But in the words of the poet, Anderson M. Scruggs,

"Yet after brick and steel and stone are gone,
And flesh and blood are dust, the dream lives
on."

"Shady ladies?" I said to Flip over the phone. "Yuch."

"Well, anyway, it proves there was a Dreamland Park and a roller coaster. And you know what? There's a picture of the duck pond. The same bridge and everything. And the tennis clubhouse hangs out over the pond just like the dance palace did in the picture. And there was a roller coaster. A big one."

"Somehow, I can't picture a roller coaster in Dunthorpe," I said. "In Indianapolis, maybe, but not Dunthorpe."

"Well, I'm telling you it was there, and, if we did a little archaeological spadework, we might come up with some fresh evidence of our own." So from that day on, we referred to the duck pond as Dreamland Lake, but we didn't get around to archaeological spadework until early spring.

It was still basketball season, which took up most of our time. I was the tallest seventh-grader, and

Flip was the fastest on his feet. So we had to go out for inter-middle-school basketball. But we were on the bench a lot. Even though I was the tallest, guys a head shorter could outjump me. And though Flip was the fastest, he had no sense of direction at all and often dribbled right up into the bleachers.

It didn't matter much, though, because the coach saw we weren't going to be big-time high school material. He concentrated on working up the better players and kept off our backs. "You two have got the natural advantages," he told Flip and me, "but you'll never do anything with them."

So on a mild afternoon in March, Flip and I avoided the gym altogether after school and headed out to Dreamland Lake. Out to where we found the dead man.

Two

We stood on the bank of Dreamland Lake, comparing the present with the picture in Estella Winkler Bates' book. The cast-iron footbridge over the middle part of the lake was pretty much the way it always had been. From a distance. But now, Park Department sawhorses blocked off the approaches to it on each side because the floorboards were rotted out. The porch of the tennis clubhouse sagged over the south shoreline and needed a coat of paint bad. And back where the roller coaster had been, a jungle of trees and undergrowth had taken over. A few mallards V-ed across the lake in our direction on the off chance we'd brought bread crumbs.

We walked our bikes around the shore to where a path dipped down into the woods, following the creek that fed the lake. At first, it was like a tunnel of branches, so we left our bikes and went on, bent nearly double. It was damp-smelling and dim inside the woods. Flip sat down on an old concrete block to get his bearings.

"We haven't explored in here since we were kids and didn't know anything," he said. "According to the picture, I figure we're right about where the roller coaster was. We ought to be able to find part of the foundation or something. They must have had to sink some kind of supports for the superstructure."

"You're sitting on one," I told him.

He jumped up and looked at the concrete thing. Then in his Sherlock Holmes voice, he said, "You know, Bry, I think you're right for once." He jumped up on it. "This is one of them! Look—right between my feet is a hole where the wooden beam went in. And straight up, maybe a hundred, maybe a hundred and fifty feet. And the track on top of that! And those cars roaring down. Boy! Think of it!"

"Yeah, well, we never got to ride on it," I said. In the seventh grade, I had the idea that all the parties were over and we'd been born too late.

"Come on," he said, jumping down. "If we locate all these supports, we'll be able to trace the route of the roller coaster. If they're all this big, they still ought to be above ground level." We found another concrete block, covered with moss and tipped at an

12

angle, beside the creek. And, on the other side, another one. I jumped the creek to get to it, but Flip was talking as he made his jump and landed with one foot in the water.

It didn't slow him down any, though. "We'll just get a rough idea today and come back with graph paper and make a ground plan. It must have been a big devil." He was plowing on ahead of me, kicking through the piles of wet, dead leaves.

Then I heard him say, "Shoes . . . a pair of shoes." He was standing still, ankle-deep in the leaves. Before I caught up with him, he'd whirled around facing me. "Behind me," he said in a funny, tight voice. I couldn't figure out what had come over him. "Come on," he said, "we're getting out of here." But he didn't move. And neither did I.

He was swallowing air fast and breathing, "Jesus, oh Jesus." I looked past him and saw a pair of shoes sticking up out of the leaves at a funny, splayfooted angle. They were leaf-colored and round-toed like old construction boots. They didn't make any sense to me. I kept staring while Flip kind of half turned and tried to get another look out of the corner of his eye. Underneath the leaves, past the shoes, I saw what looked like a pile of old clothes. And farther up something else, something shiny.

There was a breeze that whisked the leaves around a little. I was staring at the shiny place, and then, right away, I was looking at a grin. A big, yawning grin right down on ground level and a black eye socket. A leaf was over the other one. And some hair on the clean, white bone of a skull's forehead. I looked at it with both eyes, and Flip looked with one. It was a dead man, but I didn't know it at first.

The parts seemed all disconnected. Some of it just looked like rags on the ground, except for the grin. I kept looking at it, and my mouth was open like the dead man's. Then I saw one of the teeth in his jaw was gold. I knew then what I was looking at. I heeled around in slow motion and took off running back the way we'd come.

And when I came to the last concrete block we'd found, I flopped over flat on it and threw up in the creek.

DUNTHORPE MORNING CALL

March 22

LOCAL YOUTHS FIND VAGRANT'S BODY

Two local boys playing in the wooded, marshy area west of the Marquette Park duck pond discovered a badly decomposed corpse late Tuesday afternoon.

Alerted by the boys' parents, the Police Department made investigation and have cordoned off the area to discourage curiosity seekers. Black Hawk County Coroner V. H. Horvath estimates the middle-aged male may have been dead for as long as three months. Police Chief Ross H. Heidenreich speculates that the man was a vagrant of the type who still follow the disused right of way of the St. Louis, Effingham & Terre Haute Railroad, running along the northern border of Marquette Park. Coroner Horvath has called an autopsy "well-nigh impossible" and has declared the death to be of "presumed natural causes."

The youngsters, Philip Townsend, 12, son of Commander and Mrs. Wilmer Townsend, 134

Oakthorpe Avenue, and Brian Bishop, 12, son of Mr. and Mrs. Murray Bishop, 243 Oakthorpe Avenue, are students at the Coolidge Middle School.

Though Chief Heidenreich holds out scant hope for a positive identification, he calls for the cooperation of any persons who may have pertinent information.

DUNTHORPE MORNING CALL

March 24

LETTERS FROM OUR READERS

Sirs:

I feel confident that I speak as the voice of the total Dunthorpe community when I point the finger of scornful accusation at the municipal agencies clearly and wantonly derelict in the duties for which they are more than amply paid.

The Park Department receives our most ringing condemnation for allowing a deceased individual to lie unburied so that *innocent children* at their play are compelled to look upon the *Awful Face of Death*. Any such traumatic experience may well lead to the most *damaging* future consequences in unformed minds. Furthermore, the Police Department deserves official reprimand for turning a Blind Eye to the hordes of tramps and hobos allowed to roam at large within our city limits to trespass, steal, and insult womanhood.

I consider it the civic duty of this newspaper to print my letter in its entirety as a call to action in a community whose public services are a Notorious Outrage and whose children face a clear and present danger.

(signed)

(Miss) Bernadette Dunthorpe
Number 1 Dunthorpe Boulevard
Dunthorpe

Dear Editor:
This letter is about your article in the Wednesday *Call* that tells how Brian Bishop and myself found the dead man.

We were not "playing" in the woods west of the duck pond like you said. We were doing historic research into the roller coaster that used to be there when the duck pond was called by its right name, Dreamland Lake. If you knew Estella Winkler Bateses book on this subject, you'd know this was Dunthorpe's own Coney Island in the old times.

I'm not twelve years old. I was thirteen Monday and Brian Bishop will be thirteen in one week.

Yours truly,

Philip Townsend
134 Oakthorpe Avenue
Dunthorpe

P. S. Also, Brian Bishop's mom called the police when he got home. My mom didn't. I did.

P. T.

If you can't guess who the Celebrities of the Week were at Coolidge Middle School, you're no judge of human nature. Even eighth-graders were asking who we were. Flip got most of the glory, though, because my mom made me stay home from school the next day. She said I'd have to get back on my feed and have a better color before I could go out and face my public.

But unburied cadavers aren't what you'd call a dime a dozen in Dunthorpe, so the school was still in a mild uproar by the time I got back.

On Friday, Arlene DeSappio passed me a note in Language Arts that said, "What's it like to look at the Awful Face of Death?" I drew crossbones and a skull with one big tooth on the back of her note and passed it over to her, and she said, "Oh, wow!" and gave out with a little scream and a giggle.

Which was unfortunate, considering it was Language Arts. The teacher for this was one Miss Mabel Klimer. She believed strongly in Written Expression but she hated note-passing. A point spaced-out Arlene never could grasp. Also, Miss Klimer never had liked Flip from the first day, and I don't know why.

She didn't have much of an opinion of me, one way or the other. But on Dead Man Week with everybody making a big deal out of Flip and me, she more or less associated us with the cause of the excitement. And she hated any kind of an interruption. What she thought of Arlene DeSappio is another matter. But Arlene's scream and giggle was Miss Klimer's last straw. She stalked over to the board and started to erase the Quotation for the Day. It was:

To Braggarts and Gossipers
This proverb does appeal:
The steam that blows the whistle
Will never turn the wheel!

But then, she took another look at this, decided it still applied, and left it. And right next to it, she wrote in large printing:

DEATH BE NOT PROUD, THOUGH SOME HAVE CALLED THEE MIGHTY AND DREADFUL, FOR, THOU ART NOT SO, . . .

She turned around to the class as if she'd just made a major point and stared right at Flip, who hadn't been doing anything. Then, she let her look drift over in my direction. The idea was pretty much lost on everybody anyway, since no one ever connected Miss Klimer's Daily Quotations with real life.

So, generally speaking, we were a big deal with everybody but the teachers that week. Even the coach gave a little locker-room speech in P. E. about how goof-offs who cut basketball practice even at the end of the season are liable to get into big trouble, develop dirty habits, and grow up ignorant about team spirit.

But it wasn't how the public reacted that counted with me at the time. Like Miss Klimer always said, FAME IS FLEETING. What mattered was that in a funny way it really made friends out of me and Flip. It wasn't a friendship that lasted long. And it had a bad ending. But it came on strong then. Always before, we'd just been two kids who hung around together as much as possible. Showing off for each other's benefit and pretending to be as grown-up as we could. And that's all there was to it.

The showing off and pretending didn't let up much, but finding the dead man changed things.

Even before we took a notion to turn the whole thing into a big, faked-up mystery fantasy, things began to change. It was a pretty sickening experience, especially for me. But something came out of it. Before I'd finished heaving up in the creek, Flip took charge. He walked me home. I was scared and embarrassed, and probably a little mad that Flip hadn't started throwing up too.

But he never said anything. He took hold of me by the arm with one hand and walked my bike with the other. We had to circle Dreamland Lake and go up a hill past the tennis courts and down a long sloping part of the park to where Oakthorpe Avenue dead-ends. He left me at my back door and put my bike away in the garage.

I was still staggering around and maybe crying a little, but he just said, "Go on in the house and tell your mom. I'll see you later."

Then the next day, back at school, he never told anybody about me being sick. He had a good chance to, since I wasn't there. And not only that. He could have gone around telling how he discovered the body first, which he had. But no, he always said that *we* found it. It was a little thing, but it made a big difference to me at the time.

The next week we took over Wally Myers' paper route officially. Wally figured he'd outgrown it since he was about ready for high school. He'd been sub-contracting the Sunday delivery and weekly collections to us all year anyway; so, we were groomed for the job and ready to take it on as a partnership by ourselves. Besides, carrying a paper route spelled the end of basketball practice.

With all this going on, it took me a few days to

remember another point. I asked Flip about it when we were delivering papers one day. "How'd you get your bike home that day?"

He knew right away what I was talking about. "After I walked you home, I went back and got it," Flip said, sending a paper straight up onto Mrs. Riordan's porch roof and then sending another one up in the general area of her front door.

"You went back there?" We'd left our bikes outside the woods, but still I thought it took guts to walk back that close to the dead man—with nobody around and evening coming on.

"Sure," Flip said, kind of cocky, like he was talking to one of our temporary fans. "Why not? I didn't want it swiped." Then, as though he just remembered it was me he was talking to, he said, "I grabbed it and tore-ass out of there without looking back. I was home before you got your back door open."

Then he gave out with a kind of a snort and a grin. And for the first time, we could relax about the whole thing.

Three

At that age, you're glad for any excitement that comes your way. Before Flip and I had our adventure, I always liked trying to fit myself into any TV plot that showed a little action. I remember this show I saw once that left a big impression on me.

Two sadistic big kids kidnapped this younger one and hid him in a cave. It was just for kind of a sick joke—not for ransom or anything like that. Anyway, this young kid was being held underground, chained to a stake, with nothing but a little pan of water and a dish of cat food—something grotesque like that

And the big sadists were just planning to leave him there a few days.

But typical of TV, there was a mining company nearby that started doing some dynamite blasting for a highway. So, the kidnapped kid was either going to be blown up or buried permanently. Or both. Anyway, he was saved by the highway patrol, or the Texas Rangers, or some Long Arm of the Law who dug him out at the last minute.

Shows like that always knocked me out. Like how I'd feel if I was in this kid's situation. Now Flip, watching the same show, would either call it crap or think up some foolproof method of escape for the buried kid. Even though my mind never worked that way, I was always right in there anyway, putting myself in the middle of the drama.

But the dead man was about more than I could handle. There's nothing like reality to ruin your taste for TV. By Friday night, I was starting to dream about him. Bordering on thirteen is a bad age for nightmares. Too old to yell for your parents and too young to get up and have a cigarette for your nerves.

Besides, if I'd had a cigarette, its smell would have brought my mom out of a deep sleep and straight into my room. Then we'd have had a real-life nightmare on our hands.

The dream started out clear as anything with Flip and me walking around the edge of Dreamland Lake. Just like it happened, except the path into the woods was all lit up with weird green lights, flashing and throbbing. We'd get nearer and nearer to the tunnel of branches. And I'd be in two places. Walking along with Flip, but standing way back at the same time, watching both of us—trying to yell out, DON'T GO IN THE WOODS. DON'T LOOK.

But then the scene would shift, and I'd be in bed in my room alone, knowing I'd been having a nightmare but thinking it was over. And I'd realize that something was wrong. The room was too dark.

There was something at the window, cutting down on the moonlight. And without looking at the window—without chancing it—I'd know somebody was outside hanging onto the side of the house staring in. I didn't have to look to see the moon shining on the top of the smooth skull or catch a glimmer from off the gold tooth. I knew HE was there, staring in. Then he'd put his hand against the window.

Except, it wasn't a hand. It was just a bunch of bones. And they'd start pushing against the window pane. Except, it wasn't glass. It was like plastic—like one of those dry-cleaning bags. And the dead man's hand was pushing against the window, which was beginning to give. And I realized he could break the window and nobody would hear because it wasn't glass so it wouldn't shatter. And I couldn't move. I couldn't move because I was pretending to be asleep; except, I wasn't. I was dead or as good as dead.

Then somebody is standing right next to my bed, and I figure THIS IS IT. Except, the dead man is still outside the window, taking his time about getting in. And this somebody standing next to my bed is whispering something into my ear. And I'm trying to hear because maybe this is somebody who can save me. So I strain my ears trying to hear. And this terrifying whisper comes back: "I am Estella Winkler Bates. And I could help you, if I wanted to."

Then I'd really wake up. But I was in the same

room as the nightmare so I couldn't be sure it was over. I'd lie there sweating and wanting to go to the bathroom, but not going because bed seemed a little safer. Then I'd calm down and drift off to sleep. And there'd be a rerun of the same dream again. I must have gone over it two or three times in one night— like Ebenezer Scrooge on Christmas Eve.

So on Saturday morning, I was so tired that even getting out of bed was a big deal. But I did. And first thing, I went over and touched the window to see if it was real glass—just in case SOMEBODY had switched it on me and put in a pane of silent plastic.

Waiting for Saturday night was almost worse than The Dream itself. I better explain the deal Flip and I worked out about Sunday morning delivery. On Saturday, the *Dunthorpe Evening Commercial* was always thin—down to twelve pages. But on Sundays, the *Commercial* combines with the *Morning Call* in a big, fat supplement—with a four-color comic paper, and a Society Section, and the *Family Weekly* magazine. And it had to go out before dawn.

Since you had to be at the drop-off by four on Sunday morning, Flip and I made a deal about alternating Sundays. That way, we didn't both have to get up and deliver the Sunday edition every week. It was typical of my luck that the Sunday after the dead man was my turn.

Usually, I'd turn in early and set the alarm for three-thirty. But that Saturday night, I knew the minute I'd turn off the lights and slip into bed, it'd be OLD BONES AT THE WINDOW all over again. So I horsed around the room while my mom yelled up every once in a while to stop prowling and get some sleep. The third time, she yelled, "Your father is starting up the stairs."

I doubted it, since he's not the family disciplinarian. I flipped off the light anyway and made a dive for the bed. But I definitely decided not to sleep. It'd be more restful just to lie there and think than to have old Estella Winkler Bates hissing in my ear. And that must have done the trick because the next sound I heard was the alarm going off.

I was dressed and nearly down to the corner before I realized I was out alone before daylight. It never had bothered me before, even though I wasn't ever in love with carrying forty pounds' worth of Sunday paper around in the clammy cold. But that morning, I was looking behind every bush and tree. At first, it felt creepy when I thought I was the only person awake in Dunthorpe. Then I was hoping I really was the only person awake in Dunthorpe. The street lights were still on, and the trees made jerky dancing shadows on the sidewalk. And I started jogging—partly to keep warm.

They'd already dropped off the bundle in front of Walgreen's Drugstore. I was just ready to drag it back into the doorway to roll the papers when I realized I'd forgotten to bring my wire cutters. So I lost ten minutes, fiddling with the wire that binds the pile so tight it usually cuts the top paper in half. And trying to get the wire untwisted with hands I couldn't keep steady, I drew blood a couple of times and wiped it off on my windbreaker because I didn't give a damn.

The Sunday delivery's a grind—not even counting that you have to get up in the middle of the night. The bike's useless because the load's too heavy. And there's an unbreakable rule against throwing the paper up on the porches because it might disturb the subscribers' sleep. So you had to carry the papers around in a canvas bag, and you had to walk up every set of porch stairs, and you had to lay the paper right down in front of the door.

One of the customers, Old Man Sanderson, was always up already, waiting for the paper. He stood right inside the front door and watched you every step of the way, to make sure you brought it up to the door and didn't throw it, which wouldn't have mattered anyway since he was already awake. But if you did throw it, he turned right around and called the paper, and they issued you a "complaint referral." So you might as well walk up and lay it at the old devil's feet because that's what he wanted, and he didn't get his kicks any other way.

I was starting off on the route, and the sky was getting a little gray in the east, which somehow just made everything spookier. There'd be these sudden gusts of wind like little cyclones of leftover leaves, making me think of the dead man. Everything did.

The route starts with Union Avenue, which has a lot of old, gray, frame houses leaning toward each other right next to the sidewalk. My dad used to say they'd been a string of sporting houses until my mom said she didn't see any reason why sporting houses needed to be mentioned. Now, they're divided up into apartments so I could unload three or four papers on each porch and get the load down to where I could handle it better.

Then you crossed a sort of invisible frontier and made a sharp angle onto Prairie Avenue. This is sort of old-time, classy Dunthorpe. Not as classy as Dunthorpe Boulevard, which wasn't on our route, but classy enough. Big houses here, strung out with long lawns divided by hedges that made me a little nervous. The porches were dark. At the old Smythe place, the wind was making the porch swing squeak back and forth—like something invisible was sitting out there, catching a breath of early morning air. I skimmed the paper across the porch floor there without coming all the way up the steps.

It was between the Smythes and the Garrison place that I began to think somebody was tailing me. I stopped, but I didn't look back. I thought I heard a couple more footfalls, but then they stopped too.

To make things worse, the Garrison place was the biggest pile on the block—with a drive curving around the house and a garage way back behind it with rooms up above for the chauffeur. He took the paper too, so you had to walk way back in there between the hedges.

Usually, this was my favorite part of the route because Old Lady Garrison had this classic Lincoln Continental that stood out there in the drive ready to take her to church. Not that Old Lady Garrison knew she had a classic car. She may have thought it was still new. There were always plenty of rumors about her, which I tended to believe at the time. Like she was off her head and that the chauffeur had to dress her—talk like that. But she had a claret-red, mint-condition, 1947 Lincoln Continental. Usually, I took a break then and just ran my hand over the sweep of the fenders and dreamed about driving it.

Not that morning, though. She could have had a museum-quality, 1930 straight-eight, 145-H.P., boat-tailed Packard Speedster in fire-engine red, and I wouldn't have given it the time of day.

I started back toward the street. But Old Lady Garrison's driveway was crushed white rock so it made noisy walking. When I got around to the front of the house, I stopped and looked up and down

Prairie Avenue. It was just daylight. As far as I could see in both directions, nobody was around. So, I crunched on out the drive to the sidewalk. Just as I came around the hedge, somebody who was squatting down behind it stood up—about a foot away from my right ear.

It was Flip.

Not that I knew him in the first second, though. I jumped up in the air and came down with a grunt of real terror. Papers went all over the hedge. And the minute I saw who it was, I could have pushed his sassy face in. But he just said, "Thought you might like a little company this morning."

Then he took the papers for the other side of the street, and we were done in half the time. I didn't say much. Being Flip, he had to stage something dramatic, like making a sudden appearance. But then, he knew I'd be glad he was there after the first shock wore off. What can you do with a guy like that? I never could handle him.

It was when we were on the way home and the sun was up that Flip gave me the second scare of the day. The Catholics were already out, on their way to seven a.m. Mass at St. Anthony's. It was a nice, bright Sunday morning. I was even considering telling Flip about my nightmare of OLD BONES AT THE WINDOW with the hope that maybe he might have had a restless night or two himself. Though I doubted it. When he said in his off-handed voice, "I been thinking we might have another look at the woods."

I tried to let this pass, figuring he was just fooling around to see how chicken I was. But you never let things pass with Flip when he had an idea. And this was a serious one. So I cleared my voice, which at that age was jumping around like crazy anyway. "Why?" I croaked out.

"Well, for one thing, we never made our survey of the roller coaster pilings. Not an accurate one."

"To hell with the roller coaster," I said.

"And for another thing," he said, "I'd like to photograph the site."

"What site?" I said, as if I didn't know.

"Where we found the body."

"I hadn't heard tell the Police Department had hired you on as official photographer."

"Very funny," he said. "As a matter of fact, Dunthorpe's fuzz probably never even thought to photograph it. They're not extra bright, you know. They don't even pick up on what you can learn from TV."

I'd had this feeling that maybe Flip was holding a grudge against the police for easing us out when it came to their investigations. Flip wasn't a full-scale —what's the word?—*exhibitionist*. But it had crossed my mind he wouldn't have objected to a little more credit where credit was due. Maybe our pictures in *The Morning Call*—something like that. It was still eating him. After all, how many kids that age do you know take the trouble to write letters to the editor?

So I knew right then that, sooner or later, he'd have both of us slogging through the spooky woods, reliving the whole thing. I made up my mind I might as well try to play it cool and go through with it. But I thought it was ghoulish, and I told him so.

Of course, he was ready with an answer all thought out that stopped me cold: "It'd only be ghoulish if the body was still there, which it isn't. Besides, we're not going to wait till Halloween and go back there at the stroke of midnight or anything. We're going back in broad daylight and maybe take a few pictures for kind of a souvenir about what happened. Besides, that's what you're supposed to do."

"Says who?"

"Says anybody who's been through something like that. If your horse throws you, you're supposed to get right back on him and ride to prove you can. Otherwise, you might get a complex."

"Like starting to have nightmares about it?" I said casually, looking the other way.

"Yeah, like that," Flip said. "I can picture yours now in full color with sound effects."

Four

It wasn't more than a week before Flip brought his camera to school one morning. He was carefully stashing it away in his locker before First Period. Then at lunch, he said, "Old Elvan Helligrew's taking our route this evening." So I knew this was The Fatal Day.

That afternoon, I dragged my feet considerably the whole length of Marquette Park, trying to get Flip interested in other points of local history. When we came to where the old race track had been, I tossed out the idea that we might plot its course.

"It was supposed to be a half-mile track," I said, trying to sound like Flip when he's in one of his teaching moods. "If we could figure out exactly where it was, we could use it for jogging . . . work up to a couple of laps a day or more . . . be good for us . . ." I let my voice tail off. It was useless. Volcanoes suddenly erupting wouldn't have put Flip off his stride.

But when we came up over the rise where the lake was and my stomach began to get that sickish feeling again, I happened to notice that the door to the tennis clubhouse was standing open. I put on my normal voice as a kind of a last-ditch effort and said, "Hey look, they must be getting the clubhouse opened up for spring. Let's us go over past there and see if they've put the coke machine in yet. My throat's a little scratchy." Then I coughed a few dry coughs to prove the point. Flip gave me this knowing look, but we headed around the lake that way and up to the clubhouse. It wasn't anything more than a delaying action. We both knew it.

But the minute we got to the clubhouse door, we could see they hadn't even started fixing it up for the season. It was just one big room—dance floor size— and we could look across to the French doors that led out to the porch overlooking the lake. They were bolted shut, and the rest of the windows still had their winter shutters on.

No coke machine yet, either, so I was willing to give up, but Flip said, "Something funny about this. Look, the door's been forced." It had. The padlock was still closed, but the hasp was ripped out of the rotten wood on the doorjamb. The bent-up nails were scattered around on the front step.

I wouldn't even have noticed it. But Flip was giving it his private-eye look. It gave me the creeps. And for a minute there, I'd just as soon have headed on into the woods. But we charged into the clubhouse, you-know-who in the lead.

At first, it looked like nobody had been there since fall. Last year's unburned newspapers jammed into the big rock fireplace, and all the empty lockers for the tennis players' gear standing with the doors open. It had a pretty abandoned feeling about it.

Flip was all over the place at once. "Take a look at this," I heard him say from over in the far corner. He was squatted down in front of the giant roller they use to smooth and level the clay courts. It was propped up in the cobwebby corner. There was a thin crust of dried clay on the roller part. Somebody had scratched a swastika on it, with a pocketknife, probably. One of those crooked crosses like this 卐, that the Nazis used to use for their emblem. "It's fresh," Flip said. "Look, you can see the crumbs from the clay on the floor there. Somebody's been carving on this recently." I about half-expected him to take out a clean envelope and sweep the crumbs into it for laboratory analysis.

"So what?" I said. "This whole place is carved up with initials and dirty pictures and all kind of stuff like that."

"But not with swastikas," Flip said. "And what about those?" He nodded down at the floor. There, on both sides of the roller, were candles stuck onto the floorboards in their own wax. They were burned almost down to nubs. Black candles. Talk about weird. We just stared at them awhile. Then I muttered, "It's almost like an altar."

"Yeah," Flip said, "like it meant something important to somebody." He reached into his pocket and fumbled around through all the portable junk he carried with him and came out with a book of matches.

"Let's forget it," I said, but he was lighting the candles. When they began to glow, the front of the roller brightened up and the swastika stood out. It was even carved down into the metal part—very careful work with little flourishes that the candlelight picked up. It was like something in an old World War II movie—down in a bunker or something. But it was more than ever like some evil kind of altar.

"I'm getting out of here," I said.

"Two of us," Flip said. He stomped on one of the candles, and I stomped on the other one. And we made our exit through the clubhouse door at the same time. It was good to be outside, even with the woods that close.

In a way, The Mysterious Nazi Altar took the edge off my fear of going into the woods. "Bunch of little kids fooling around in the clubhouse," I said, for an easy explanation.

"No. That's not anything little kids would think of," he said. And then, we were in the middle of the woods, almost at The Spot. "I should've brought my light meter," Flip said, acting a little too easygoing, I thought. He was fumbling with the camera case, supposedly deciding on the shutter setting in the little clearing where we'd found the dead man. Neither of us looked right at the spot.

But if we were going to take a picture of it, we were going to have to locate it. In the clearing, you could still see where the cops had tramped all over the leaves and weeds. When we saw there wasn't really anything else left, we got brave. "Stand right on the spot, right where his feet were," Flip said. "I'll take your picture, then you take mine."

The truth was I couldn't be sure where the dead man's feet had been, and I was just as glad. So I picked a spot at random, without looking straight down, and Flip didn't challenge it. He just snapped the picture. Then we changed places, and I took his.

After that, we didn't quite know what to do with ourselves. I guess what we actually wanted was to relive a piece of the excitement without the full hair-raising effect of the first time. But instead, we were just standing around in the woods, and it was like nothing had ever happened there. So Flip said, "I hope I remembered to turn the film. Maybe we better take a couple more shots just to be on the safe side." So we did. It was still a letdown, but I was feeling pretty good anyhow. Flip was probably right about climbing back on the horse, so to speak.

The sun was getting low by then, and I think he and I had the same thought at the same time. Maybe it would give us a charge to hang around the woods as it got dark. We were in the mood for a little mild spooking. So we wandered back to the roller coaster block, the one next to the creek I'd flopped on. Flip chose this to sit down on, which I didn't particularly appreciate. But he didn't say anything, and I sat down beside him. We started talking about what they'd probably done with the dead man's remains. Flip thought the County must have buried him in the graveyard out at the Poor Farm.

I gave out the opinion there wasn't enough left of him to fill a box; and so, they probably cremated him. Flip thought this was possible, and that got us to wondering if they'd yanked out his gold tooth before they disposed of him. Flip thought it would make a pretty good ornament for a key ring or a watch chain or to hang around your neck on a lanyard. So, as the conversation went on and the sun went down, we managed to give ourselves a little minor thrill or two.

We were getting each other worked up pretty good and decided to tell *Dracula*. We hadn't told *Dracula* in maybe two years. In grade school, that never failed to get to us. Sometime around fourth or fifth grade, I'd slept over at Flip's house one night. They showed *Dracula* on the "Creature Feature Midnight Matinee of Horror" on Channel Twelve. The real, original, black-and-white version with the horses pulling the carriage turning into bats and the whole bit.

But it was no good. We'd outgrown it. Instead of scaring each other like in the old days, we kept arguing on the details of the plot. Finally, Flip said, "I guess we might as well head home. I've got to see the Nitwits get their dinner." The Nitwits are Flip's three younger sisters. His dad's in the Navy and away most of the time and, when his mom was out playing golf or something, he had to ride herd on the Nitwits. This wasn't his favorite duty, but I'll tell you one thing: when he cracked the whip, the Nitwits jumped.

So we got up from the roller coaster block. Flip picked up his camera case and was just about to swing the strap over his shoulder when he froze and whispered, "Jeee-sus!"

Now this was more or less what he'd said when he'd found the dead man. And it scared me so bad I nearly wet my pants. Then I thought he was trying to pull something on me. But he wasn't.

He was staring at the concrete block we'd been sitting on. And right where our bottoms had been, there it was—another swastika. It was carved just about as carefully as the one in the clubhouse, but deeper and bigger. The concrete was kind of porous, so the detailing wasn't as good. But it had taken somebody quite a while to do. Painstaking wedge-shaped cuts. It was a wonder we hadn't noticed it before we sat down.

"Hitler strikes again," Flip said finally, but his voice was shaky.

"That wasn't there the other day," I said. "We'd have seen it."

"I know."

Then a kind of hissing, swishing sound made us look up. We could see a flash of white through a break in the trees over by Dreamland Lake. One of the big swans was soaring in an arc up over the water, like something had stirred him up. He was moving his big wings in a slow, easy motion. Like a large albino bat.

"Home," Flip said. And we hustled out of the woods, very close together.

The other ducks were kind of agitated by the big, swooping swan. They raised an unearthly racket, squawking at each other and swarming out of the water and up on the grassy bank. We were watching them as we walked along the shore path. They were tame as anything and waddled along ahead of us like a bunch of little old men.

So they got to the barricade closing off the condemned footbridge before we did. And they all waddled over something lying right in the middle of the path. At first, it looked like a stick that had fallen there, but when we got up close we saw it was a long, skinny, leather pouch with a little flap at the top fastened shut.

"Now what," I said, as Flip picked it up.

"I don't know, but something's inside it." He unfastened the flap, and there was the handle of something inside. He let the leather sheath fall. And then he was holding the wickedest-looking knife I'd ever seen. Polished to a high chrome finish and razor-sharp.

If knives are your thing, this one was a beauty. It was like a bayonet, and the handle was perfectly shaped for a good grip. Flip stood there holding it and gawking, completely dumfounded—a look he generally tried to avoid.

"This is worth something," he said. "Get the leather thing." We walked off, and he held it away from himself. It was one mean-looking weapon. "It'd cut your damn fingers off if you took hold of it by the blade," he said.

Up by the tennis courts, we sat down on the bleachers they have there for tournament time. Flip laid the knife down between us. "Look, we both found it so it's ours, but I'll take it home."

"How'd we come to that decision so quick?" I asked, even though I figured it would naturally stay in Flip's possession.

"Because if you take it home, your mom will find it. And if I take it home, my mom won't." It was as simple as that. My mom notices everything. His mom notices nothing. "Slip it back into the holster or whatever you call that leather thing," he said, "but be careful."

Then we made our final discovery of the day. Right on the handle where Flip had been carrying it, there was a design worked into the black wood. It was getting toward evening, so we had to bend over it to see. There was a little wreath of leaves, very tiny and intricate. Inside that there was an eagle, looking to one side, with stiff, straight wings. The eagle was perched on a little round thing like a ball or a circle. And inside the circle—you guessed it—another swastika.

"Is that . . ."

"Yeah, it sure is," Flip said. "And this one's the real thing. I mean it's a real Nazi relic from Germany." He was standing up and sort of hopping around in excitement. "From World War II or before. Authentic."

"But what's this all about?" I said. "There aren't any such things as Nazis anymore. They lost the war. Besides, there never were any in Dunthorpe. Couldn't have been."

"That's what you said about the roller coaster," he said, giving me this keen, squint-eyed look, "but there was."

And so we started off home, feeling like we'd gotten a little more than we'd bargained for out of that afternoon, but not being sure what. When I turned in at my house, Flip said, "Not a word about this—to anybody." And I gave him my if-you-can't-trust-me-you-can't-trust-yourself look.

Then he went marching off down Oakthorpe Avenue with his camera swinging around his neck and the Nazi sword held out in front of him—heading home to feed the Nitwits.

Five

If they had their supper that night—the Nitwits, I mean—they got it on the table themselves with no supervision from Flip.

When I walked in the back door, my mom greeted me with, "You're in big trouble. The *Commercial* called to say not one of your papers got delivered. No doubt you have a reasonable explanation." I was saved from giving it to her because the phone was ringing, and of course it was Flip.

"That damn Elvan. Bugging out on the papers. I

should've known better than to trust that fat-butt. Offered him a dollar twenty-five to do it too."

"Not in advance, I hope."

"Are you kidding. Come on. We'll have to get them out. Those subscribers'll have our heads for this."

We delivered the *Commercial* after dark that night, and just about everybody was out to greet us with a few well-chosen words. About the mildest came from Mrs. Kitty Riordan, who said to me at the same minute I was handing her the paper, "Naughty boy, where *is* my paper?" It didn't make any difference that it was right there in her hand. She had to give out with something.

But, of course, Old Man Sanderson was the real treat of the evening. There he stood on his top step, scowling out into the night. I was nominated to walk up and hand the paper to him. "Just four hours late!" Old Sanderson snarled. "That's all. Just four hours. I've called the *Commercial* six times, I'll have you know, and if I have anything to do with it, you two louts'll lose the route."

I kept trying to hand him the paper, and he kept raving. Then he jerked it out of my hand and hauled off like he was going to smack me across the face with it. I didn't flinch, but Flip stepped up behind me and said, "Go ahead and hit him, Mr. Sanderson. And I'll be down at the police station in ten minutes to tell them you knocked Brian all the way down the porch steps and probably concussed him."

Old Man Sanderson looked at Flip like he couldn't believe his ears. Then he turned back toward the door, muttering, "Damn brats. I got a good notion to call the *Commercial*."

We headed off down Prairie Avenue, and Flip said,

"You got to be meaner than they are or they walk all over you."

What you learn from a paper route. It makes you dread turning into an adult. About the only house where we didn't have to take some kind of sass was Old Lady Garrison's. Her door was shut tight with only the little light on over the door bell that nobody ever rang. We figured she probably didn't know whether it was daylight or dark.

"Wait," Flip said. "Just wait till we get hold of Elvan Helligrew tomorrow. There isn't an excuse in this world that'll get him off. None."

"Maybe he was rushed off to the hospital with the acute appendicitis," I suggested, just to whip Flip up.

"I'll take out his appendix for him," Flip muttered, "and maybe a couple of his teeth."

There never used to be anything specially strange about Elvan Helligrew—unless you're not used to his name. He was always fat, though. Not puppy fat. Fat.

But you know how it is, there's a fat kid in every class. Nobody gave him a hard time about it as far as I know. He wasn't jolly, either, like round people are supposed to be. He wasn't really much of anything when it came to personality.

Once, though, back in the spring of fifth grade when we were all kind of naive, he created a sensation in a way. It was just before school was out for vacation. We'd turned in our books and everything. The teacher, Mrs. Vogel, didn't know what to do with us. So, we had Open Discussion. She asked if any of us had any special plans about how we were going to spend summer vacation.

Right off, Elvan put up his hand, and Mrs. Vogel looked kind of startled. In this funny, high voice he had, he said, "I'm going to a trim-down camp in the State of New York."

That was a real conversation-stopper. Nobody knew what a trim-down camp was, including Mrs. Vogel. She was all set to say, well-that's-nice-Elvan, but he started fumbling in his hip pocket for his wallet, which was wedged in back there pretty tight. He took out a newspaper clipping and carefully unfolded it. It was an advertisement for a camp for overweight boys.

This place promised to trim from fifteen to fifty pounds off any fat kid who went there. They have this entire staff of medical doctors, and star athletes, and a special diet table. There was even a picture of a kid in the ad. He was holding the waistband on a pair of pants way out from his belly to show how much weight he'd lost just from going to this camp.

Mrs. Vogel looked a little bewildered. But since that was the first rise she'd had out of Elvan all year, she said, "Well, I'm sure everybody wishes you good luck in this enterprise, don't we, boys and girls?" And we all said we sure did.

Then on the first day of that next fall, we were in the sixth-grade room with a different teacher. But Mrs. Vogel came right into the room during class time and walked up to the new teacher who didn't know any of us yet. And she said to him in a fairly loud whisper, "I wonder if I could take a look at Elvan Helligrew."

But Elvan heard her, wiggled himself out of his desk, and said, "Here I am, Mrs. Vogel."

"Why, Elvan," she said, kind of embarrassed.

"I gained twelve pounds at that camp," he said in sort of a proud voice.

But on the day after Elvan didn't deliver the *Commercial*, I was a little worried about what Flip might do to him. I always thought I was a pacifist by nature. That's what comes of being the tallest kid in the class, which I always have been, but not the toughest, which I never will be. But Flip had been known to be somewhat scrappy. I wasn't worried that he'd do any real harm to Elvan exactly. It's just that it seemed pretty useless when it's too late to do any good. Why bother?

Flip caught up with Elvan in the lunch room that day. I knew he would. For once, I felt like not having lunch with or near Flip. After all, I had other friends, but I couldn't think of any at the moment.

It may have been the other way around, though. I mean maybe Elvan caught up with Flip. Anyway, there they were standing in the middle of the cafeteria, face to face and tray to tray. Flip looking mad and Elvan looking enormous.

Along with everybody else, I heard Flip call him "an irresponsible fink." And—here comes the bad part—Elvan was just nodding and saying, "I know it, Flip, old buddy. I know it. Whatever you call me is true, and I don't have no excuse." And with this sick grin on his face. Like a damn dog or something—a damn big dog that hangs around waiting for you to kick it.

You could tell this was having an effect on Flip. He was sensitive, even though maybe nobody knew it but me. It sort of took the wind out of his sails, though I'm not so sure Elvan meant it to. It was almost like Elvan wanted more punishment—and in front of the whole school for an audience at that. It made me lose my appetite.

"Well, let's forget it," Flip said, backing off. "I'll know better next time. There won't *be* any next time."

But Elvan was edging toward him with his tray piled up with double orders of everything and two desserts. For one tight moment, I figured he was going to sit down at our table. But he just hung over it, waiting to hear anything more Flip might have to say. Then he waddled off down the aisle to the last table —like a duck.

"Feel any better?" I asked Flip as he slapped his tray down across from me.

"Can it," he said and stabbed his Salisbury steak with an upside-down fork

Six

Now when I look back, I can see everything or nearly everything. It was like we were hypnotizing ourselves. We wanted some big, glorious mystery to liven up the ordinary routine a little. For awhile, we weren't admitting that we wanted to think the dead man in the woods maybe met with "foul play" as the saying goes. But we were getting there. The Boy Detectives were yearning for adventure with a big A.

Besides, there was all that Nazi junk. Pure intrigue. Better than late-night TV. We were in for a few more experiences before the last one we had together. And we were ready for anything, we thought.

Our fame at Coolidge Middle School was wearing off. The Public doesn't concentrate on any one point long, especially with Easter vacation and softball season coming on.

One afternoon, Flip and I were working the route as usual. I was delivering on the north side of Prairie Avenue, and he was delivering on the south. This was our quick-march plan for days when we wanted to finish up early and stop off at Walgreen's fountain for a coke or something before heading home. Anyway, Flip gave out with his two-tone whistle which was always our private signal. He was standing halfway up Old Lady Garrison's front walk, motioning for me to cross over.

And behind him, for the first time ever, Old Lady Garrison's front door was open. I couldn't believe it. Her chauffeur always paid us at the end of the week. So we'd always go around back to the garage to collect. The only times we'd ever laid eyes on the old lady herself were when she'd be out in her Lincoln Continental, being tooled very slowly around town. She'd sit up in the back seat like a dusty-looking statue, with a veil down covering up her face, looking straight ahead. You couldn't tell if she was cracked or not. You couldn't even tell if she was alive.

But she wasn't standing in the front door. It was Bunratty filling up the space completely. Bunratty was our own name for Old Lady Garrison's chauffeur. We didn't know his real name, but we'd gotten Bunratty out of a book we'd read part of once, and it sounded like exactly the right name for a chauffeur. So, Bunratty standing there in the front door gave me a kind of a shock, even though we'd had dealings with him before.

He handled everything for the old lady. And he knew we had this love affair going with the Lincoln. He never chased us away from it or anything. I think he figured we were respectful enough about it not to do any damage. He wasn't much of a conversationalist. He looked a lot like a bodyguard out of Chicago and possibly not too bright, but you wouldn't want to tangle with him. He had one enlarged ear like he might have been a fighter at one time, but apart from that, not a mark on him you could see.

Flip and I walked up to the front door together. When we were in the little entryway, with Bunratty looming over us, he said, very quiet, "Leave your papers out here. Mrs. Garrison wants a word with you two."

I was trying to give Flip a look to see if he knew what we were in for, but he was gazing around, dazed, as we went into the front hall. "Wait here," Bunratty said and disappeared through a normal-sized door which was cut out of two gigantic sliding doors. That front hall was bigger than a regular living room. And instead of wooden floors, there were little fancy interlocking tiles—light green and pink. And a staircase wide enough for a small car, that went up, then made a turn, then went up some more.

"She mad about the late delivery last week?" I whispered to Flip.

"I don't think so," he whispered back. "This doesn't make any sense to me, but remember, she might be . . ." Then he tapped his forehead, which didn't put me at my ease any.

Then Bunratty came back, and Flip and I bunched together. "Okay," he said, very low, "go in. But don't sit down unless she tells you to." We went through the little door in the big door, and I was hoping it would stay open behind us. But it didn't. Big Bunratty closed it as soon as we were inside.

At first, we thought we were alone and that maybe there was another door we were to go through. It was a huge room, with a regular forest of furniture. A lot of high-backed chairs and funny lamps that were on because the drapes were pulled to. Instead of having one big shade apiece, the lamps had little branches on them and a separate little pink shade on top of each branch. It was an interesting room, with a lot of rugs. Some of them overlapping. There was too much in it to describe. But we couldn't find Old Lady Garrison at first.

Then we heard one of the chairs say, "Over here, boys." It had a hollow voice. And we came around the chair, and there was Old Lady Garrison sitting, looking into a fireplace with no fire.

Old lady doesn't describe her. *Oldest lady in the world* does. She looked too old to get up. Even the crevices in her face had wrinkles inside them. She had almost no hair, but she was wearing a hair net. And some of her lunch was on the front of her dress. Except it was more like a robe that went down onto the floor. There was a red, fake flower pinned upside down on her shoulder.

She looked up at us, but I wasn't sure at first she could really see us. She looked. We waited. She looked. We waited. Then in a very clear voice, she said, "Which of you lads is Philip Townsend of 134 Oakthorpe Avenue?"

Flip was struck dumb. He stared at her and kept swallowing. "Well," she said, just as clear as before, "have you forgotten which of you is which?"

"Me, ma'am," Flip said. It must have been his first

use of the word ma'am. I never heard it from him before.

"And which of you is Brian Bishop of 243 Oakthorpe Avenue?"

"That's who I am," I said, slightly confused.

"Yes," Old Lady Garrison agreed, "you'd have to be."

Another long pause. Finally, Flip said, "If it's anything about the service, about the delivery or anything . . ."

"It's not," she said. "You can sit down." We looked around for a place, but all the other chairs seemed to be going the other way and looked too big to deal with. "You can sit on the floor," she said. "You're young."

"Well," Flip said, and his voice cracked up a couple of octaves, "we ought to be getting on with our deliveries."

"You've delivered at Sandersons already, haven't you?" Old Lady Garrison said. "Then you can let the rest wait awhile."

Along in there, I decided she wasn't completely cracked. Half, maybe.

"I understand you boys found a dead body behind Dreamland Lake."

Silence.

"Well, did you or did you not?"

"Yes," Flip and I said, like a duet.

"I thought you were the ones," she said and nodded to herself. "What did he look like?"

"The dead man?" Flip said.

"That is the topic of this discussion," Old Lady Garrison said.

"There wasn't much of him left," Flip said.

"It made me sick," I told her. I don't know why I

said it. It wasn't the kind of information I'd been volunteering during our famous period.

"Did it, indeed," she said, showing interest. "When I was a girl, I went to Dreamland Park with some regularity, though not, of course, with my mother's permission. I know the area well. How does it happen that two lads such as yourselves are interested in it?"

"We're interested in history," Flip said.

"History!" Mrs. Garrison shot back. "History! History involves the decline and fall of the Roman Empire and the Norman Conquest. We're talking about Dreamland Lake!"

"Yes, ma'am," Flip said, to cool her off.

"And you've been reading Estella Winkler Bates for your information, haven't you?"

"Yes, ma'am. It's the only book we've found."

"That girl is an absolute fool and cannot write."

"I didn't know she was still alive," I said, surprised.

"I didn't say she was," Mrs. Garrison replied. "I never rode the roller coaster," she said, looking at Flip. "It would have blown my hair. And I was subject to bilious attacks—like you," she nodded at me. "I was interested to read of you boys finding a dead body. Children are so sheltered nowadays. Even at funerals, you never get the full effect. I understand that closed-coffin services are fashionable now. How is one to understand death without seeing it?"

Silence.

"Exactly," Mrs. Garrison said, nodding to herself again and beginning to finger the flower pinned on her shoulder. "Do you see this flower? Remember it. It figures in what I am about to tell you. You will be better men for having seen death. Some persons think they will live forever. They will not. This is ignorance. Get up and go over to the piano, one of you, and bring back the photograph you find there in a Lalique frame. No, not both of you, I said one of you."

Flip went, and I stayed on the floor. But Mrs. Garrison just waited in silence. When he came back, carrying a picture, she reached out a claw and took it, holding it up so we could see it. It was a picture of a boy, sitting on a bench with one leg crossed under him. He was in short pants, maybe ten or eleven years old. "This is the best portrait of him that I have," she explained. "Though he was into his first pair of long pants when I lost him. He was my son, Oliver Hatfield Garrison, the only child I had. If he had been spared to me, he would have been a Circuit Court Judge, possibly, a State Senator today.

"Don't be restless," she said, looking over the picture at us. "This story will not last as long as you may think. In a few minutes, you will be back outside again, none the worse for this experience.

"This house was quite new when my son was taken. At his play, he ran into the street and was struck down by a milk van of the Morning Glory Dairy Company. If he had been killed outright, it would have been preferable. He lay in an upstairs room, which is untouched from his time, for six weeks and four days. He had suffered extensive brain damage. And yet, his mind was often clear. His vision, on the other hand, was not. 'Mother,' he would say to me, 'wear something bright; otherwise, I can't see you, and I think I'm alone.' And so I always did. I wore a bright flower pinned to my dress, though it was winter and nothing in the garden."

She laid the picture in her lap and put both hands

over on the upside-down flower on her shoulder. "I'm never without it."

We thought then maybe she was going to cry. So Flip said, "I'll bet he was a fine boy, Mrs. Garrison."

"He was a boy like other boys," she said. "You are the first boys in this house since he was carried out of it. You may go now. On the table next to the doorway as you leave you will find something of interest to you. Take what you find there."

Then she settled back in her chair and turned the picture of Oliver Hatfield Garrison face down in her lap.

We got up, and at the door on a little marble-topped table were two envelopes, one with my name written on it and one with Flip's.

In the hallway outside, we looked around for Bunratty, but he wasn't there. So we shot out the door, scooped up the papers, and breathed deep in the outside air. But once we got past her hedge, we dropped the papers and tore open our envelopes. There was a piece of folded-up paper in each one, with writing across it that said, "For your time." And inside each paper were two Kennedy half dollars.

We looked at them awhile, and then Flip said, "We won't spend them. We'll keep them."

Seven

It was only a couple of nights after our little visit with Mrs. Garrison that the next bombshell dropped. It must have been a Friday night because I was up roaming around my room late, wishing, as usual, for my own TV set. My mom was downstairs, in front of a talk show which comes on at the same time as Creature Feature Midnight Matinee of Horror. And according to *TV Guide*, that night they were putting on "The Mummy's Curse"—an old chestnut I never tired of. You remember, when he comes down out of his tomb and starts scratching around outside the girl's tent. That was always the big moment.

But convincing Mom to trade her nightly ritual for Boris Karloff wasn't worth trying. And she'd be tying up the TV at least until my dad got home from one of his late runs.

I ought to explain that my dad owns four big Fruehauf trailer trucks for long- and middle-distance haulage. It's sort of a small trucking company. When any of the drivers is out sick or something, my dad has to pitch in and make one of the hauls. He always complains about this, but my mom says he's happiest on the road—away from her, away from his family, away from everything. She says he's in love with The Road and can't admit it. He just says, bull, he has to take the run or have a dissatisfied customer on his hands. And that driving a big rig is hell on the kidneys.

In those days, I was living for the time he'd take me on one of his runs. The day was coming, but I didn't know it then. They have these berths the second driver can sleep in up in the cab of the truck behind the seat. This is for the all-night driving runs, and I'd been nagging Dad from the time I was five years old to take me along.

And Dad always said, "One of these days." To which my mom always replied that his insurance didn't cover a child passenger and that those big trucks are death on wheels and that she would not live with the possibility of being a childless widow. My mom talks like that when she's on her high horse.

Anyway, on the night I'm talking about, the phone rang, and it was Flip. At least, it sounded something like him. With the TV going and all, I wasn't sure at first. He sounded funny. Haunted, kind of. And the first thing he said was, "Get over here quick."

"I don't know if I can get out at this hour."

"Find a way."

"What's up?"

"I don't know. Just come over as quick as you can. I'll be up in my room."

"Mummy's Curse is on," I threw out hopefully, "maybe . . ."

"Hell with that," Flip said. And hung up.

I stepped up to the living room door, where I could see two images of an Italian male vocalist giving forth with a Burt Bacharach song reflected in my mom's glasses. As a rule, she's the severe type, but let an Italian male vocalist burst into a Bacharach tune, and she's off into orbit. I left her out in space and slipped out the back door.

Talk about moving from one world to another. The difference between my house and Flip's is extreme. At my house, everything's very orderly—chairs you don't sit in and enough wax on the kitchen floor to send you into a sharp skid. But Flip's was different. I think that was the first thing I noticed about the outside world—how different things could be no more than a few houses apart.

The Townsends' front door was never locked. In fact, it was hardly ever shut. So I just walked in. Except when his dad was home on leave, the place looked pretty casual. It's empty most of the time, with the lights always on. But there's always a trace of humanity. Like a large group of people have just gotten up and left. Since it was after eleven, the Nitwits were probably bedded down. But there was a standing row of Barbie-type dolls lined up along the old leather sofa. And an unfinished Monopoly game strung out in the middle of the floor with fake money drifting all over the room. Flip's mom was nowhere around, so I started up the stairs.

It's funny about that house. I never would have been surprised to pass a bunch of complete strangers on the stairway. It's a lot like a hotel. Flip's room was on the landing with the only door in the house that was always closed. I turned the knob. But the door was locked. There for a second, I felt like I was completely alone. I gave a couple of soft raps. Then pretty soon, I heard Flip say, down by the keyhole, "Who is it?"

"Police Chief Heidenreich," I said right back into the keyhole at him. "This here's a raid."

The door opened, Flip reached out and grabbed me in, and locked the door behind me. He looked green. I still thought it was some kind of game. At that age, it's hard to tell.

"What's happening?"

"Sit down," he said. The only thing you could say for Flip's room was that you didn't ever have to worry about messing it up. The only place to sit was his bed which was never made. It was a little rattrap of a room, and he always kept the ceiling light on. I think he slept with it on, but that was his business. He had the usual posters and stuff on the walls, but you couldn't see them because he'd screwed in a bunch of hooks for his clothes. They hung all over the room because he'd turned his closet into a darkroom. He had a drop cord with a red light bulb in there and everything.

That first minute or two had me going. I always figured I was the one who was supposed to be scared if anybody was. And he was the one who was setting it up. But then, it dawned on me Flip was scared and, for once, not trying to pretend otherwise.

Excited, though. He was standing over me, running his hands up and down the sides of his Levis, like he was cold. Finally, he said, "Remember the pictures? The ones we took in the woods?"

I nodded, still thinking I was about to be put on.

"Well, I finally finished off the roll and developed them tonight."

I'm no judge of photography. Flip never taught me anything about it because the closet wasn't big enough for two people. Still, even I knew he was no professional yet. The prints were on one big sheet, and he handed it over to me. It was kind of a senseless jumble of subject matter, which meant he'd clicked away at random just to use up the film. I could figure that out since there were so many views of the Nitwits. I ought to mention the Nitwits have their own separate names: Rita, Melody, and Terri. And most of the pictures were of them, making terrible faces at the camera and horsing around in the back yard. Then there was a shot of the Townsends' car, a Rambler American station wagon. And an artistic shot of Flip's own feet.

But there were also the four shots of the woods— two of him and two of me. The two I'd taken of him were a little off center. All four were pretty dim. There we were in the woods, though, but I didn't see anything creepy about it.

"You aren't really looking at them," Flip said. "Not with a trained eye." He was rummaging wildly around the stuff on the top of his desk, "Where's my damn magnifying glass," he was muttering to himself. "I just laid it down, and now the damn thing's gone."

Then he found it and handed it to me "Look again. Look through this. Use your eyes." Man, was he wound up.

There's this word for falling in love with yourself —your own body, I mean. Whatever it is, I don't have it. I hate looking at pictures of myself. Especially when I was thirteen—all skinny legs and waiting for acne. I was just standing there, in the picture, looking at the lens, kind of round-shouldered like I always am except when my mom's around.

But I used my eyes, and then I used them on the pictures of Flip. It was just his usual self, in the old-faithful, vinyl windbreaker and faded denims, ankle-deep in the leaves, standing on the dead man's supposed location. I had the feeling that if this was a test, I was about to flunk it.

Flip was dancing around in front of me, banging himself on the side of the head. "You're just looking at *us*," he said, like this is the last straw. "Use the damn magnifying glass, and look at the background."

It was only trees and leaves, and out of focus at that. But I made little circular sweeps with the glass all around the four pictures. The truth is you never see anything if you're not looking for it. But I kept trying to see something interesting because I had the idea Flip was about to grab everything out of my hands.

"Look," he said, flopping down on the bed next to me. "In this one, and this one too." One of them was of me, the other of him. "Look at that tree on the right, behind us. It's the same one in each shot. Look at it!"

So I put the old spyglass right over the tree and started to bring it back toward my eye, concentrating. When I got it about halfway between my eye and the snapshot, I felt something go through me. Flip was absolutely still, for once. I shifted over to the other picture and started drawing the glass back from the tree in that one. Same feeling. I was looking at something. Did I know right then what it was? If I did, I was fighting it.

"The moon?" I said, sort of clearing my throat at the same time.

"The MOON?" Flip yelled. "Are you nuts? How could it be the moon?"

There was a little semicircular white spot next to the tree, behind it, actually.

"A melon?" I said, scared now. I could feel the old goose pimples coming up on my arms.

"A MELON? JEEE-SUS!" Flip bellowed. He was about to pound sense into my head. "You know what it is! Say it! Say what it is!"

"It's . . . it looks like . . . it could be . . . a face."

My hand started shaking, so I put the magnifying glass down on the picture sheet in my lap. Right on the grill of the Rambler. We sat there, listening to nothing.

"It is a face, Bry," Flip said, very quiet. "We weren't in the woods alone that day."

"The hell we weren't," I said, trying to calm down. "It's an optical illusion. It's just a spot on the negative. You've got a light leak in your camera. It couldn't be—no, we were alone. We'd have known. We . . ."

"Oh, can it," Flip said. "We weren't alone, and here's the evidence."

Then we were quiet again, more scared than we'd been since Dead Man Day itself. Scareder, possibly. I wanted to go home, but I didn't want to make the trip. Finally, I looked over at Flip, but he was staring across the room, to the inside of his closet door which was standing open. There on the back of the door was hung the Nazi sword in its case, dangling from a hook.

The moon-melon-face-whatever was only in two of the pictures. I scanned the other two to make sure. That tended to rule out a light leak, but I was trying to pretend it was all a mistake because IT hadn't shown up in all four pictures. Flip had already been thinking about that.

"Look," he said, "somebody was standing behind that tree. Maybe he followed us into the woods—remember where we were before we went in there—or maybe, he was already in the woods and took cover when he heard us coming. Anyway, he's behind this tree, see, and pokes his head out to keep an eye on us every once in awhile, then hides again. Waiting to see what we're doing or something. So it just happened that his head was poked out while we were taking two of the pictures. Pure chance."

"Then that means" (my imagination was really getting revved up), "that whoever was there was really in all four pictures, but he's concealed in two of them."

"Yeah," Flip said, impressed. "He's right back there behind that tree the whole time."

"But why?"

"Good question."

"Now wait a minute," I said, getting businesslike with the magnifying glass again. "This is just kind of a blob. You have to use your imagination to see an eye, or a nose, or part of a mouth. It probably isn't . . . what you think."

"Well," Flip said, "one thing's for sure. You can't identify anybody from these prints. So I'm taking them down to the Camera Shop tomorrow and have them enlarged. I've always wanted an enlarger, and now, here's a time I really need one, and I don't have it. They'll get them up to a size where we can tell for sure. It'll cost a little for the enlargements, but we'll take it out of the route money." At least, this part of the evening had an old familiar ring about it. We were always deducting some expense from the route money so that we rarely had any ready cash.

I got up to go. "It's not a face," I said, not looking at the pictures, "but you'll have to have them enlarged to prove it to yourself. You're spooked, and now you've got me spooked. It's contagious spooking. But it's not a face. I've decided it's not."

"No," Flip said. "You've decided it is."

Eight

"Poetry," Miss Klimer said in Language Arts on Monday, "deals with *all* the experiences in the spectrum of life. It takes the *world* for its province. How many of you boys and girls thought poetry was only about hearts and flowers and knights in shining armor?"

None of us said anything. We didn't feel like giving her the satisfaction of the answer she was trying to drag out of us. "Come, now," she says, running her hand through her somewhat thin red hair, "I feel certain that many of you, indeed, *most* of you, have relegated poetry to a very *limited* sphere of influence in your lives. Haven't you?"

Dead silence. "Well, you have," she says, like we're giving her a big argument (which we are in a way). "And the reason is simply that you don't know that poetry *is* reality!"

Then she sort of skips to the back of the room, a little out of breath. Actually, she's old, but she tries to act like a young chick. She flips on the overhead projector that throws a poem on the front screen. Then she calls on Isabel Wilson. "Isabel, you have such a *fine* voice. Read this poem aloud to us!" So Isabel, who's the class star, does. It's a poem with no rhyme about a bunch of bulldozers wrecking a building. Or, maybe, it's about dinosaurs eating rocks. You can't tell which. And that, according to Miss Klimer, is the artistry of it.

Then she flashes up another poem which is stranger than the first one. It's got words going all over the page in little circles. You have to hang by your heels if you want to read all of this one. *If* you want to.

So Miss Klimer, who knows it, reads it to us. It's just sounds—like crash, zowie, ker-thump, and like that. Only in circles.

"Notice the *shapes* and *sounds* in this poem, boys and girls. Isn't it a *noisy* poem?"

"Yes, it's very noisy," Isabel Wilson says.

"*Very* noisy," Miss Klimer says. Flip looks across the room at me. It's going to be one of those weeks, his eyes tell me. We're anxious enough as it is for the days to keep moving, since the Camera Shop won't have the enlargements ready until Thursday. We kind of wondered how we'd be able to wait that long.

But Miss Klimer is saying, "Now starting tomorrow, I want each and every one of you boys and girls to find a poem on his own. A poem you will read aloud to the entire class. A poem that deals with the *reality* of today—no hearts and flowers and romance, now. Remember, a poem takes the whole world for its province."

Isabel Wilson puts up her hand, "Would you say, Miss Klimer, that poetry is universal?"

"Oh, yes, Isabel, oh, yes, indeed, I would. Well said."

So on Tuesday, since we're good little middle-class children . . . and since most of us would rather keep Miss Klimer off our backs even more than we like to give her a little trouble . . . well, because of these things, most of us turn up with poems.

"Now then," she says to start the class, rubbing her hands together as though we're all really going to enjoy this. "Who will be the first to share with us a poem he's discovered?" Her eyes flit around the room, looking for somebody likely.

Isabel's raring to go, of course. She ruffles the pages of poetry she's copied out to show she's got quite a lot to choose from and wouldn't mind being called on more than once. Isabel wasn't as bad as she sounds, by the way. It was just that she didn't see herself as a student. She saw herself as the Assistant Teacher. Outside of class, she was easier to put up with.

"Well now, Isabel, I think we'll just save your selections until last so we'll have something to look forward to." Isabel nods like this is probably psychologically sound.

And I put my hand up. This freezes Miss Klimer's eyes in midflit. I'm not what you'd call an aggressive participant. That means I never volunteer. But I have a poem, and I'd just as soon get it out of the way so

I can relax and think my own thoughts. And providing I can pick it out myself, I don't mind poetry—rhymed or unrhymed—it's all the same to me. What I do mind is being addressed as "boys and girls."

"Brian Bishop has a poem," Miss Klimer says, like she's not so sure I do. "Stand up and read it to us." So I do. I'd found it in a fairly new book, and it met all the requirements. It was very modern and up-to-date, and it was all about a high school band marching down a street in the fall—very moody, and with sound effects, and quiet after the band goes off in the distance. Short too. When I finish it, Miss Klimer looks pleased—and somewhat relieved. So I sit down, and Miss Klimer starts looking for the next victim. Arlene DeSappio has her hand halfway up, but Miss Klimer's looking everywhere but at her. She calls on a few more boys and girls, and they give theirs.

By then, Arlene is waving her hand in the air, and so Miss Klimer says, "Yes, Arlene, now you."

So poor old Arlene jumps up and starts in without even looking down at her page. In this high, fast monotone she recites:

Sunset and evening star,
And one clear call for me!

which brings on sort of a groan running through the half of the class that had Mrs. Vogel back in fifth grade. This happened to be Mrs. Vogel's favorite poem, and she made us all memorize it. But Arlene plugs along with it like it's hot off the presses and way up on the charts.

And may there be no moaning of the bar,
When I put out to sea, . . .

The nearer the end, the faster she went. Arlene was developing a very good bosom. But from the neck up, she was lost. When she finished, she dropped back into her chair, kind of flushed.

Then Miss Klimer says, "Yes . . . well, that was, of course, a poem highly praised in the last century. And certainly very well known . . ." Then she gives up because we all get the point except Arlene, who's looking bewildered because she'd been aiming to please. "Well, let's move right along. I wonder if *you* have a poem, Philip Townsend?"

He does; and he gets up, and comes to the front of the room, and announces the title: "Frankenstein."

Then he begins, sort of acting it out with appropriate gestures of one hand:

In his occult-science lab
Frankenstein creates a Flab
Which, endowed with human will,
Very shortly starts to kill.
First, it pleads a lonely life
And demands a monster-wife;
"Monstrous!" Frankenstein objects,
Thinking of the side-effects.

Chilled with fear, he quits the scene,
But the frightful man-machine
Follows him in hot pusuit
Bumping people off en route,
Till at last it stands, malign,
By the corpse of Frankenstein!

Somewhere in the northern mists
—Horrid thing—it still exists . .
Still at large, a-thirst for gore!
Got a strong lock on your door?

This performance is met with a long ovation from the class, who never counted on any entertainment in Language Arts. They love it. And as Flip returns to his seat, people reach out to shake his hand and ask him for a copy of it and like that.

When it's finally quiet, Miss Klimer draws herself up extra tall and says, "When we speak of modern poetry, we do not include *morbid doggerel.* That so-called verse is, among other things, tasteless. I do think, Philip Townsend, that you have a twisted sense of humor and a preoccupation with the grotesque. Isabel, I think we need you, read some . . ." But the bell rings then. And Miss Klimer sits down, completely disgusted, as we all try to see who can get out the door first.

That's pretty much the way the week went. But on Thursday we quick-marched through the route, hurling papers at porches with wild abandon and bad aim. So we were downtown at the Camera Shop just before it closed.

"Game of hide-and-seek?" said the guy behind the counter, who'd been looking at the pictures. He pulled the enlargements out of a big manila envelope. We'd had them blown up to eight by tens. I was trying to elbow Flip out of the way so I could see them, but he was jamming them back into the envelope and paying the clerk.

"Come on, Flip, let's have a look at them," I said as he was taking giant strikes down Market Street. "Not here," he said. "Someplace where we can concentrate."

We could either go to The Napoli for a soda, or we could take the bus home. Finances didn't cover both. "To the Napoli," Flip said, so I knew he couldn't wait, either.

The Napoli was empty at that time of evening. It smells like chocolate syrup and has the reputation of doing a little quiet business in the narcotic trade. But it has big, high-backed booths, and it's about the only place where you can sit down in privacy.

"Come on, cut the build-up," I said.

"Order first." So we ordered—the usual: all-chocolate sodas with sprinkles. And two waters on the side

"Now," I said.

"Now." And he began to pull the pictures out of the envelope slow and easy, trying to drive me crazy. He acted like he was going to keep both of them, but, at the last second, scooted one across the table at me

So we both look. My stomach's turning over. We exchange them and look again.

Then we look at each other. "Might have known," Flip said finally.

It was clear as anything. In both pictures. The face looking out from behind the tree belonged to Elvan Helligrew. A big, round moon-face.

I should have been relieved. At least, it wasn't some mad monster or a stranger. It was, at least, somebody we knew. Somebody harmless. And I should have been mad too. Since, instead of taking our route for us that day, Elvan had been stalking us through the park, poking his nose into our private business. But I don't know. I still had this weird feeling. In a way, I felt embarrassed for Elvan for doing it. And too, I still felt insecure. Like we thought we were alone, but we weren't. Like you're always at the mercy of somebody or something that's watching when you're not. But instead, I said to Flip, "Well, that clears up the mystery."

"Part of it," he said. Then the sodas came.

We had to walk home, but the days were getting

longer so it was still light. In the distant past, we'd done some jump-riding: leaping up on the back bumper of the Number Five bus and hanging on for dear life. But we'd outgrown that. I was tall enough so they'd see me through the back window from inside the bus.

I could take longer strides than Flip, but he walked faster to make up for it. We headed off past the Public Library and out West Jefferson Avenue which finally ends up at the entrance to Marquette Park. But we turned off and cut across the campus of the Bible College before we got there.

Along in through there, Flip said, "I wouldn't have thought he could manage it."

"Who?"

"Elvan, who else? How'd he go creeping along within a few yards of us without us hearing him? Size he is, you'd think he'd sound like a rhinoceros battering down a jungle."

"Light on his feet, I guess. He's spongy "

"Yeah, like a dirigible."

We were just coming out of the other gates of the Bible College onto West Monroe Street, which is the quickest way home, when Flip said, "Well, I hate to have to do it, but we've got to be nice to Elvan."

"I'd hate to have to do it too. So why?"

"Why? Use your head. We've got to find out why he was in the woods. We've got the evidence." He waved the manila envelope. "Now we got to get to the motive."

"We've already got to the motive," I said, trying to get the upper hand. "I can give it to you in a nutshell. You remember the next day, when you took after him in the cafeteria about not delivering?"

"Yeah."

"Well, you remember how he acted. Like he *wanted* you to call him every name you could think of. Like, maybe, if you started slapping him around, he wouldn't have minded that, either."

"Yeah, well, that's the way he is," Flip said, kind of ashamed-sounding.

"And that's the way he's always been—long as I can remember—always wanting attention, always wanting to hang around with some gang or other. Nobody'd ever have him. Listen, in the middle of that whole thing in the cafeteria, he called you *old buddy*—OLD BUDDY—get it? He doesn't care what he has to do to get in with us—you, especially."

"Good luck to him on that."

"Good luck nothing! According to you, we're going to be nice to him now. We'll be stuck with him till high school graduation. Maybe longer. Just so you can find out what we already know. You better realize, when we start being nice to him, it's not going to be easy to get rid of him."

"When did you take up practicing psychiatry?" Flip wanted to know. "You'll be charging thirty-five, forty dollars an hour to shrink people's brains before we know it."

"Yeah, and you'll want to go into partnership with me, so we'll be broke all the time same as now."

"Well, I'm not saying you're wrong. But you're overlooking a few points."

"Such as?"

"Such as what we found in the tennis clubhouse. And what we found carved into the concrete roller coaster thing. *And* what we found by the bridge, which is hanging up on my closet door and is authentic."

He had me there. I'd have gladly forgotten those

Nazi souvenirs. "What's that got to do with Elvan?"

"Maybe nothing. Maybe something. We've got to find out, don't we? We've got to get into his confidence. Then if we find out he didn't have anything to do with that part of things, well, then we'll have to turn our investigation in a new direction."

"Instead of turning our investigations in new directions and spending the rest of our lives with Elvan Helligrew and all those fun things, I got another idea," I said. "We could forget the whole thing."

"Could we?" Flip said.

Nine

If it'd been left up to me, all I'd have done was just go up to Elvan and say, hey, we might as well be friends. To start the ball rolling, what could be easier? He'd have jumped at it. Of course if it *had* been left up to me, I'd never have gone near him. But since it was Flip who was managing things—as usual—it had to be elaborate. And, as Miss Klimer would say, "preoccupied with the grotesque."

He was still carrying around *A Centennial History of the City of Dunthorpe, Black Hawk County, and*

Environs. He kept renewing it at the library, even though we didn't have much time to continue on our local history kick. The librarian must have been overjoyed to have old Estella Winkler Bates off her shelves all spring.

So one day, while we were making the deliveries, he started carrying on about the Municipal Art Museum—not one of our regular hangouts. He must have been reading up on it in study hall. "Built as a palatial residence by Marius Benderman, drainpipe and ceramic tile tycoon, in 1878," he quoted, more or less from memory.

"No kidding," I said.

"An eclectic structure, basically Italianate, with the popular Gothic embellishments of the period. Wagonloads of tourists came to watch the construction which took three and a half years."

"Do tell," I said.

"The central staircase—entirely black walnut—was handcarved by Bavarians and rises from the reception hall, connecting with a conventional box staircase to the central tower."

"Think of that," I said.

"There's a statue of Diana Undraped—Goddess of the Hunt—in imported marble in a niche in the sitting room."

"Diana Undraped—right here in Dunthorpe," I said.

"Built as a country villa, it now stands near the middle of the city on eight landscaped acres, only a fraction of its original grounds. Dedicated to the people as an art museum in 1914 by the Benderman family."

"A pleasant parkland," I said, "where once gracious living of a bygone day still hangs around. Thank you, Estella."

"Oh, shut up," Flip said.

So after we got the papers out, we walked over to the art museum, which is in a neighborhood that's known better days. Basically Italian with Gothic doodads it may be, but it looks like the chamber of horrors today. Old Marius built big, but it lacks the homey touch. The only thing that kept it from coming off like a Halloween card was that, now that it's an art museum, they have fluorescent lights hanging down from all the ceilings. This doesn't add to the charm, but it does give it a modern, everyday glow. We went in.

"Herringbone parquet," Flip said, pointing to the floor of the entrance hall. It was put together with little pieces of polished wood in a zigzag pattern.

Just to keep up, I pointed out the staircase and said, "Handcarved black walnut."

The art exhibit was of local talent. And since there isn't much, nobody was looking around, and most of the walls were bare. "Let's find Diana Undraped," I said, but Flip was heading for the handcarved staircase.

"I wonder where the curator is," Flip whispered.

"Beats me," I said. "In fact, I don't know what one is."

"That's the person in charge," he said, "like the caretaker. And from now on, keep quiet."

So I could see we were up to something even before Flip started creeping up the stairs, which were carpeted, luckily. The only art on the second floor landing was an oil painting of Marius Benderman with a beard down to his belt. The staircase went on up, but there was this little velvet rope across it with a sign: PUBLIC NOT ADMITTED BEYOND THIS POINT. Flip went under it. I went over it.

The third floor landing was smaller, with five closed doors. Dark too. Flip looked at each one of them and, finally, pointed to the only one that had a little step under it. He tried it, and it opened.

"Conventional box staircase leading to central tower," I quoted to him.

"I said be quiet," Flip whispered back. He hustled up into the complete darkness. The steps were uncarpeted and steep. We were both going up on hands and knees. I thought I better pull the door shut behind us, just in case. So it was like the middle of a moonless night. The staircase made several turns, but, finally, we came out in a little room. Dusty as hell, with cobwebs. We were standing in the top of the tower right over the front entrance of the museum. There were narrow, round-topped windows on three sides. You could see all over town. We were up, maybe, five floors, and you could look over the trees downtown to the Merchants' and Farmers' Bank Building, which is the local skyscraper.

"Great view," Flip said.

"We're trespassing," I said.

"This'll do just fine," Flip said, and started off back down the stairs. We got all the way back to the second floor before we heard voices. A bunch of women were just coming in the front door. So we whirled around and contemplated the painting of Marius Benderman. Then we strolled back down the stairs like a couple of well-known art lovers. And out the front door.

I didn't bother to ask Flip why we'd done it—or why it would "do just fine." I was always supposed to be able to figure out ahead of time what we were planning. And I wasn't about to ask.

The next day at school we were about the last ones through the cafeteria line. Flip had told me to wait for him, and he arranged to be late. So the only table left was the one at the back. It was sort of Reject's Row, if you know what I mean. Elvan was there.

Flip made a line straight for it. When Elvan saw us flop down within easy reach, he looked up from his mountain of lunch, and his face really lit up. But right away, Flip started talking to me in an extra loud voice. Like we were in a play or something. But also like we were completely alone at the table.

"Well, Bry, tonight's the night. Yessir, this is the night we've been waiting for. Going to go down to the art museum just as quick as we get the papers out. I hear you can climb right up into the tower if you go up the main staircase without getting caught. Then you go through this door and up some more stairs, and there you are. Supposed to be the best view in town, they tell me. 'Course, it's strictly off-limits. I don't know if we better risk it. Still, it's worth a try. Never been up in that tower, have you?"

"Sure," I said, And Flip gave me this look like I'd gone berserk and betrayed him. He started kicking away at me under the table. "I was up there two, maybe three, years ago," I said, very cool. "Great view. Wouldn't mind having a look at it again." At least, this stopped the kicking. I wasn't about to give Flip complete control over the conversation—once I figured out what we were up to.

"Yeah, well, we ought to be up there by about five o'clock, wouldn't you say?" While he said this, he kept an eye on me.

"I'd say so." Then we started talking about something else, I forget what. Elvan could hardly eat for straining his ears.

We were a little ahead of schedule arriving at the art museum. It was just four-thirty. And there were some bona fide art lovers wandering around the first floor. So we made a quick run through the rooms legally open to the public. It must have been a great old place in its day. As big as Mrs. Garrison's house. Without all her furniture, and lampshades, and things, it looked even bigger.

The exhibit of local talent was mostly wishy-washy watercolors—a lot of pink barns, and tree limbs, and like that. Except for them, it was an interesting place. Diana Undraped was standing up on her toes, naked as a skinny-dipper and snowy white. Somebody had painted the little alcove behind her like a blue sky with big, white, puffy clouds that were beginning to flake. And you could see where they'd had gaslight fixtures coming out of the walls in the old days. It was a nice piece of local history, and you could tell that the old ladies going around on canes and looking at the watercolor barns were glad to see young fellows taking an interest in art.

But Flip was working our way back to the entrance hall. We stood around in there on the herringbone parquet till nobody was around. Then he was up the stairs—two at a time—around the landing, and under the velvet rope. One minute, we were there; the next minute, we'd vanished. Like a couple of bats heading for the belfry.

Up in the tower room, it was still afternoon. The sun was streaming in at a low angle. All the west windows in town were bright orange. "Keep an eye on the front gate," Flip said, "but don't let yourself be seen." We stood up there maybe twenty minutes.

Then, way down in the distance, we saw Elvan Helligrew coming through the big wrought-iron gates out by the street. He was looking first one way and then the other, like we might be hiding behind the trees in the yard. But he came lumbering on up to the house and disappeared right under our feet onto the front porch.

"Behind the door," Flip muttered. The tower room wasn't any bigger than a freight elevator, but the door to it was extra wide. We pushed it back and fitted in behind it with space to spare. And it seemed like we were back there another twenty minutes. "That idiot probably got lost," I finally whispered.

But right then, we heard a sound at the bottom of the box staircase. This time, Elvan did sound more like a rhinoceros. I think he tripped and fell up the steps once, from the sound of it. But then, he began creeping on up. And the higher he got, the quieter he was. He must have stopped when his head was level with the floor, trying to see if we were up there. But then, he brushed right past the crack in the open door without seeing us. He must have pretty well filled up the doorway. Then it sounded like he walked over to look out the window. Maybe he thought he was early or maybe on a wild-goose chase.

Flip began pushing the door to, very slowly. It didn't squeak, which would have been a nice, eerie touch. It just began to swing shut. And it closed before Elvan whirled around and saw us standing there.

"If it isn't Elvan," I said.

"If it isn't Elvan, what is it?" Flip said.

"Gosh, old buddies," Elvan gasped.

Ten

That was the great beginning of our temporary friendship with Elvan Helligrew. I wish it had stopped then too. I wish that more than anything.

Flip scared Elvan halfway out of his skull that afternoon in the tower. I forget the exact words, but there were plenty of them. He didn't bring up the woods, but he told Elvan he was sick and tired of him tailing us night and day, and how we couldn't do any exploring ANYWHERE without Elvan butting in, and it was going to stop and stop beginning now. Maybe he threatened to chuck Elvan out of the tower window just to insure our future privacy. I forget. But it was like that.

Elvan ate it up to the last crumb, nodding to Flip to keep him going until I wanted to puke. Seemed like it went on into the night, and the end of it was, okay, if we can't get rid of you, we might as well make up our minds to put up with you, but watch yourself and don't take anything for granted. And maybe we'd drop over at your place one of these days if we got invited, but don't keep dropping into our lives unless asked.

It had an overwhelming, double-barreled effect on Elvan—he enjoyed every bit of it. The humiliation, he expected. But the half-assed promise of buddyhood had him about dancing around with joy. Enough to shake the tower loose from the rest of the building.

All this led us, after a very few days, to Elvan's house. You know how there are some people whose houses you can't imagine? I mean if they have a home life, you can't picture it? That's the way it was with Elvan in my mind.

The Helligrews live in a section of town called Beechurst Heights, which is in our end of Dunthorpe, only farther out—almost in open country. It's the newest section—small-scale suburbia. One of those instant-class developments where they give each house model a special name. Like AUTHENTIC EARLY CALIFORNIA SPANISH EL RANCHO and STRATFORD-ON-AVON AUTHENTIC OLDE ENGLISH TUDOR. According to Elvan, his house was AUTHENTIC EARLY COLONIAL CAPE COD SALT-BOX.

Now that we were all three buddies, he invited us over one Saturday afternoon. Frankly, I could have passed up the invitation with pleasure. We were leading him on, and, maybe, he knew it and didn't even mind. I mean it's either friendship, or it's nothing.

Anyway, the minute we walked in the door, I knew it was going to turn out to be a bad scene. There was Elvan, slicked up like we were company. And his mother hovering around in the near background.

I guess I expected her to be another mountain of flesh. But she wasn't. She was kind of a nice-looking woman—regular size, and she's so glad to see us you could bust out crying. How nice to meet Elvan's friends, and she was preparing some very tasty snacks for us, and their home was our home. It was pretty hard to take. And it had an effect on Flip too. He was extra polite to her. After all, there wasn't any getting out of it at that point. When adults get into the act, you tend to lose what control you have.

But Elvan wanted us to himself and took us up to see his room. Which was like a picture of what a boy's room is supposed to look like. Plaid curtains on the windows and the same plaid stuff on the bed. And a nice cork-tile bulletin board—pretty empty. All very neat except for candy wrappers on the floor around the bed. Apart from them, there wasn't much evidence of Elvan in the room. "This isn't my real place," he said. "I have another place which is really my real place. I'll show that to you after awhile."

Along in there, I began to have this feeling that maybe it was Elvan who was running the show and Flip and I were the ones being sort of maneuvered.

Elvan couldn't wait to show us what his real place was, though, so right away, he started herding us downstairs. His mother cut us off as we were trooping past the kitchen, with Elvan like a big hen trying to keep us in line. He really was showing signs of taking over.

But she said, "All right now. I know boys. They're always hungry. You three young fellows just step right into this kitchen and see what's on the table for you. I have to keep your strength up, you know." What was on the table for us young fellows was a three-layer chocolate devil's-food with fudge exterior icing and interior divisions of marshmallow cream. Three chocolate malteds straight from the blender. And a fancy glass dish full of chocolate-covered peanuts. The only thing she'd left out was cocoa.

It was a pretty gross display, and it explained quite a bit about Elvan's physical condition—maybe, even his emotional state. But it was too tempting to pass up. We sort of fell for it. That woman knew how to bake. And she stood around beaming while we dug in. But the funny thing was—Elvan didn't have any appetite. He kept saying things like, "Aw, Motherrrr, we guys have got other things to do."

And she kept pinching his ear, and getting cute with him, and saying, "This doesn't sound like *my* boy." It about put me off my feed. But since Flip was telling her what good cake it was—and it was— I kept on eating.

By the time we'd polished it off, Elvan was starting to quiver. He was getting wild to have us finish up and start moving. And finally, we got away from the table after we promised Mrs. Helligrew we'd be back for seconds since she didn't seem to want to put away what was left of the devil's food.

"Come on," Elvan said, very impatient. He was beginning to bark. "I want you guys to see something down in the basement." And he pounded off down the steps, looking back to make sure we were following.

The first thing we saw was a ping-pong table, and Flip said, "Look, Elvan, we haven't got time to play—"

"We're not playing any ping-pong. Come on." He led us around behind the furnace and the washer-drier. And there was another door. On it was printed a hand-lettered sign that said KEEP OUT OF ELVAN'S PLACE. He had a padlock on it. The key to it was hanging on a chain in one of the fat folds around his neck. Flip and I gave each other a look and a shrug. We stood there like a couple of clods while Elvan fiddled nervously with the key and the lock.

He pushed the door open and started in, but said, over his shoulder, "Just hold it right there until I find the string for the light." He came right back with the end of a string in one hand. "Okay, you two, just step inside the door, and I'll turn on the light." We were inside with the door shut behind us before he pulled on the string. He was really paying us back for that scene in the museum tower—whether he knew it or not. Then the light went on.

The only thing I really enjoy remembering about that moment was the look on Flip's face. But being able to remember it doesn't mean I can describe it. I don't even know how I had the time to glance at him.

When the light went on, we were looking directly at a Nazi flag—full size—nailed up on the far wall of a little laundry room with no windows. On either side of the flag were crates or something all covered up with bright red cloth. On top of each of them were styrofoam heads—like those stands women buy to put their wigs on when they're not wearing them. And on these were German helmets from World War II—real storm trooper helmets, the kind that dip down over the ears. They looked like two cutoff heads at a human sacrifice. And they were sort of turned like they were looking at the big red, white, and black Nazi flag with the swastika in the middle of it. Underneath it was one of those artificial wreaths that people leave at graves on Memorial Day.

That was just the beginning, though; it was sort of the centerpiece for the room. On all the walls were pictures and medals pinned up. One of the pictures was of Hitler and his girl friend. He was wearing German-style shorts, and she was laughing, and they were playing with a dog. It was a picture cut out of a magazine, but somehow, down there, it looked like a personal family portrait.

The walls were full of stuff like that. Hanging down from the ceiling were little scale models of Stukas and Messerschmitts and all kinds of out-of-date German fighter planes, dangling there in frozen aerial combat. It was like going back thirty years in time. On the wrong side.

We just stood around with our mouths open—completely forgetting the big point: that this was another piece of the puzzle right there ready to fall neatly into place. The effect on us must have given Elvan a deep and satisfying charge. Finally, he said, very modest, "Well, this is my place."

For once, I had to step in and do the talking. I did the best I could. "Well, Elvan, this is quite a collection. Yessir, you must be pretty proud of it."

"It's a few things my dad brought home from the war. He's not interested in them, though. The flag and the helmets and a few other pieces. But I got most of this stuff myself with money I saved and trading with other collectors. I bought most of the medals." He was puffed up to half again his size. And standing sort of stiff with his heels together.

"I guess they must be pretty valuable by now—historic stuff like that."

"I'd never sell them," he cut right in. "I might trade up on a few pieces and duplicates, but I'd never just sell them. I keep them for my own self and to show to a few friends."

I had the feeling we were the first friends to view the collection. For one thing, if anybody else had seen it, word would have got around. For another thing—what friends?

"People didn't understand the Germans," he was saying in a high whine. "You don't get a true picture from what they write about them over here."

"Over where?"

"Over here. In this country. That's always the way when a country wins a war. They discredit the losing side. This always happens after wars. If Germany had won the war, it'd have been a different story."

"No question about that, Elvan," I said. Flip just stood there.

"Look, I wouldn't let anybody else, but you guys can try on the helmets. Here, let me . . ."

"I don't think so, Elvan." Flip had finally found his voice—it was a smooth, soothing voice. "You just leave them right there on those . . . heads. They look real good there. Let's just leave things like you got them fixed up. Like a display in a museum. It's interesting that way . . ."

"It's not just a museum," Elvan said loud. "It's more than that to me. You guys can understand, it's like . . ." Then he just stopped and looked at us. With his eyes bright, but tiny, in his big, round face. It was like he suddenly had a bad speech impediment that kept the meaning from coming out. There was some kind of a war inside him—not World War II. Something more personal to him.

We told him we had to get down to the pickup and get the papers out, and he didn't try to hold us up. We got out of there as quick as we could.

And as we were heading down the front walk, fast, his mother came out on the front step and yelled, "Remember, our home is your home!"

"Jeee-sus," Flip finally said, when we were half-way out of Beechurst Heights, "talk about sick! That guy . . ."

"It's what you were looking to find out, wasn't it? Like this solves everything, and we don't have to turn our investigations in new directions."

"Yeah, well," he said.

"Yeah, well, shut up."

We didn't talk about it for maybe a week. Finals were coming on, and we were about to leave the seventh grade behind us for good.

It was coming around to locker-clean-out day. We'd spent the week since that Saturday at Elvan's keeping clear of him. It's not hard during the school day since he's not in any of our classes, and he's excused from gym. And we could bury ourselves at a crowded table during lunch.

Then one evening, Flip called me up after supper. "Look, we've got to do something about Elvan before school's out, and we've got to talk it over first."

"So talk."

"Well, it's about the sword we found. It's his, of course."

"Yes."

"And that day, he dropped it down where he knew we'd walk by and find it."

"Probably."

"What do you mean *probably?*"

"I mean, yes, I think he did."

"Got any idea why?"

"It's my same idea that starts you off calling me a doctor of psychiatric brain-shrinking."

"All right, I won't. Just say your theory."

"For the second time, my theory still is he wanted to get us to notice him, and that sword was a real attention-getter. Besides that, it's something that really means a lot to him. It's his own private treasure. It was like an offering to us. Like here's something really great I'm giving you—now like me."

"Okay, that's good," Flip said. "But how come he's so carried away with all that Nazi crap?"

"Now you're getting off the point."

"Well, okay, if I am. Give your theory about that. I know you've got one."

"I've been thinking about it," I said.

Silence at the other end.

"I've been thinking maybe he admires the Nazis because he thinks they were supermen, which is what they thought themselves."

"And?"

"And he's not a superman. He's an unsuperman. He's a zero. It gives him something big and impressive to be a part of."

"But what good's that if nobody knows?"

"We know."

"Yeah, but what good is that going to do him?"

"Well, indirectly it's already got us over to his house, which nothing else in the world would have done. You saw how even his mother was overjoyed to see us."

"Okay, they're both weird as hell. But how about the swastika carved on the concrete out in the woods?"

"Easy," I told him. "He got all excited about us to begin with because we found the dead man in the woods. That's the sort of thing that might get him all fired up—almost like we live a real exciting life, and things happen to us. So after it was all over, he probably went down there to where the body had been and carved the swastika to kind of be in on it himself. I mean anybody interested in the Nazis has got to be interested in death and like that. Besides, he probably figured we'd go back there sooner or later. He probably even figured that's where we were going when you hired him to take the route that day."

"Maybe so," Flip said, "but how'd he know we'd go into the tennis clubhouse and find the candles and all?"

"Look, I don't know. For all I know, he planted a lot of stuff around in the hope that we'd find it and get curious. Maybe there's lots of other clues he put around we didn't even come across. I mean, once he gets something in his mind, he goes all the way. You can see that. Besides, maybe he gets his kicks by scratching swastikas around on everything. It'd figure."

"Well," Flip said, like he was giving it all his serious concentration, "your theory's good as far as it goes, but . . ."

"Dammit, that's what you say about all my theories. I think it goes far enough, and, if you ask me, I think we've gone too far. How much farther do you think the theory ought to go, Mastermind?"

"Maybe just one more step," Flip said.

"Which is?"

"Which is—maybe he wants us to notice him because he's got something to tell us. Like he was trying to tell us something that day at his house. Maybe he has something specific he wants us to know."

"Such as?"

"Such as he knows how the dead man died."

"Oh, no," I said. "Don't give me any of that. You're going too far as usual. You hate to see the end of anything, so you're dragging it out. Next thing, you're going to say is he . . . I don't know what you're going to be saying next."

"Yes. Maybe he did it. He's nutty enough to," Flip said. "Maybe he really did. With his little sword."

We wrapped it up in brown paper, the Nazi sword. And we addressed it to Elvan, and propped it up outside his locker on clean-out day, and left it there. It was like buying him off. I wish we had.

Summer

Eleven

Summer always reminds me of our swimming coach, Ralph Harvey. It always reminds me of Flip's dad too. Not that he was around in the summers much— or ever. Flip was born in the Canal Zone down in Panama. He was very proud of this little-known fact. But he couldn't remember a thing about the place.

When we were in the grades though, he used to give me this business about palm trees, and monkeys throwing coconuts, and boa constrictors wrapping themselves around the house down in sunny Central America. But we outgrew that fantasy. When he was a little kid, though, his family lived all over the country at Navy posts where his dad was stationed—Norfolk, San Diego, Great Lakes—all those port-type places.

One time, I asked Flip how come he and his mom and the Nitwits lived in Dunthorpe, which is about as landlocked a place as you'd ever want to see. He said that one day his mom announced she was moving herself and the kids as far from water as she could get. So they came to Dunthorpe. His dad turned into a long-distance commuter—except he wasn't home more than maybe a couple of times a year.

You'd have to understand Flip's mom to figure out how she came to this decision. Though I don't think anybody could ever understand all of her. Like most mothers would say, I wanted my children to have a nice, settled life in one place. I sacrificed everything for them. Sentiments like that. But she never said any of those things. In fact, she never said much of anything. She just kept to herself a lot of the time and let Flip run things. The one point you could be sure of with her was that she liked a quiet life.

Which nobody in that family got when Flip's dad, Commander Townsend, was home. When the Commander was on shore leave, all hell broke loose, and everything had to get ship shape on the double. He actually said things like NOW HEAR THIS.

I think they all counted the days until he went back to his ship or wherever. Especially Flip. I never even heard him mention his dad's name unless he was at home at the time, when it was impossible to overlook him. But I didn't give him much thought until one time in the summer after fifth grade, when we were still kids.

Those were the days when Flip and I were both

junior members of an organization called the Oak-thorpe Avengers. In a way, that's how we got friendly in the first place—by being on the lower fringes of this gang, which was run by older kids and met in Wallace Myers' garage.

To get in the gang you had to know three dirty jokes nobody had heard before. And after the initiation ceremony, when you told the jokes, it was all pretty much downhill. There weren't any other gangs in convenient, nearby neighborhoods, so we didn't have any territorial rights to defend or anything. Like all gangs, it was organized boredom. Anyway, that's how Flip and I first got to be friends.

At the beginning of that summer, Commander Townsend was home on leave. And he about had a coronary when he found out Flip couldn't swim. A Navy man's kid that can't swim! It was an outrage, and besides everybody's supposed to know how to swim because it's easy as walking, nature's best exercise, and it could save your life. Especially, if you're in the Navy.

He issued an order to Flip that he'd take him through a crash course in elementary swimming at the YMCA while he was home on leave.

And Flip, who didn't take commands very well even back then, said he'd learn to swim on two conditions. First, that the Commander wouldn't teach him —that he'd have a regular swimming coach instead. And that he could bring a friend along—me, as it turned out. This must have caused a major battle, because the Commander doesn't like anybody else's ideas nearly as well as he likes his own. It runs in the family.

But since learning to swim was the important thing, he said he'd have to let Flip have his way about it because he didn't have all summer to argue. And that's how we happened to take lessons at the Y.

The Commander took us down the first day to get us signed up. There were regular group classes, but he said they weren't good enough. If the Commander wasn't going to get to teach us, he wanted another expert who'd give us his full attention. You could tell it really got to him that Flip had ruled him out.

They set us up with an individual coach and said we could start right away. So the Commander plunked down the money for ten lessons and free swim periods. And much to Flip's disgust, he marched right into the locker room with us and started tearing off his clothes. "Dad, we've *got* a teacher; they said so. That was the deal," Flip said under his breath. But the Commander just kept flinging off his clothes and throwing them into a locker.

"Don't worry about it," he said, fiddling with his shoelaces, "I'm just going to have a quick dip. I'll be at the deep end. You tadpoles will be down in shallow water. You don't even have to let on I'm your father." The Commander had a very red face but a white body—in fighting trim, of course. He invited us to sock him in the belly if we wanted to, so we could see how tight his muscles were. We didn't want to.

You swim naked at the Y—regardless of age. And we were in our modest period—undressing close up to the locker and taking our time about it. The Commander finally got tired of waiting for us and bounded off to the pool. He was up bouncing on that board before we had our socks off.

I always remember the smell of that locker room—chlorine from the pool and the breathtaking whiff of used jock straps from the gym. We paddled through the tray full of stuff that's supposed to ward off athlete's foot; and then, we were in the big room with the pool. Cracked cement walls and big signs that said ALWAYS SWIM WITH A BUDDY.

The Commander had done a couple of quick laps by then and was at poolside doing a few squat-jumps to get the rest of the kinks out. Our coach was a guy named Ralph Harvey, and Flip's dad was telling him all about the Navy and generally lording it over Ralph—to not much effect.

Ralph became our hero that summer. We were at the age for one. He was just out of high school, but, to us, he was a total grownup without the usual annoying adult traits. To show his teaching status, he wore a pair of rubberized shorts—the kind you wear at a swimming meet. And the whistle hanging around his neck was nestled into a healthy growth of chest hair. Right away, we were impressed. While the Commander performed several dozen trick dives, Ralph worked with us in the three-foot end—with his back to the board.

He was what I'd call a great teacher. He put us through the paces, but he never pushed us too far. By the end of the session, we were shoving off from the side of the pool with our feet and floating on our backs.

On the way home, the Commander said he supposed Ralph would do. He suited us fine. In fact, that summer became the time of the Great Ralph Harvey Adventure Saga. In the pool, Ralph was very methodical—as we moved from the back float to more advanced stuff and finally onto the board. He didn't have much to say, which gave our fantasies about him a kind of a free-form quality. We nearly got thrown out of the Oakthorpe Avengers because of too much talk about our close buddy, Ralph Harvey, and what a great guy he was. How any day now we'd be taking off on a camping trip with Ralph to Canada, or maybe Tibet.

Since we didn't have anything to go on, we'd spend most of the days wondering things like if he had a girl and a car. Then we agreed that he didn't have a girl, but he did have a car. Then we had to decide what the best kind of a car for Ralph would be. But we couldn't ever settle on one particular model and body style with all the class and speed a guy like Ralph would just naturally need.

Then we wondered about his future. There wasn't any doubt in our minds but what Ralph was destined to be a lifelong swimmer. After all, we'd never seen him dry. So we debated about whether he'd keep an amateur standing for the Olympics or turn pro. Which led us right into picturing him as a Big Ten college coach just about the time we'd be entering the university—where we'd all three swim our way to varsity victory. Since we were just out of fifth grade, these were our first definite college plans. We never wondered if Ralph had parents or anything like that. His life seemed too perfect for that.

So after we'd pretty much exhausted the present and the future of the real Ralph, we decided to write a book about him—just a private one. Flip was to work out the basic plot, and I was to look up all the difficult spelling. We'd more or less talk through a chapter walking home from the Y after a lesson. Then we'd retire up to Flip's room and get as much down on paper as we could before I had to go home for supper.

Our first chapter started out with Ralph on the Riviera, lolling around on the beach wearing his usual elastic trunks and whistle. When all of the sudden he hears these screams for help way out in the ocean. So like a big jungle cat, Ralph's on his feet and running in long, easy strides into the surf, cutting through the water, straight for the screams.

It's got to be a girl, of course—with cramps. And she's out there gasping her last, with the old killer sharks circling in for the finish. Ralph puts the lifesaving headhold on her and starts for shore with these long, easy strokes. She's in a coma, of course—and a bikini.

But Ralph hears the motor of a big boat churning water. It's the girl's father's yacht. So Ralph tows the girl to the yacht, eases her up on the deck, and gives her mouth-to-mouth resuscitation (that's the first word I had to look up), while her father stands by in a blue blazer and white slacks saying, "Stranger, I don't know who you are, but save my girl, and the world's yours."

Well, then the girl comes to, and the first thing she sees is Ralph bending over her. And her dad says to Ralph, "Name it and you've got it: my yacht, my Cadillac Eldorado, my daughter. Name it, and it's yours because you've saved her, and I'm in your eternal debt."

But Ralph stands up, looks back to shore with these keen eyes he has, and says, "It was my duty to save your daughter, mister. But I have another duty to myself—I've got to be free!" Then without another word, he dives off the yacht and makes for the Riviera shore with these slow, easy strokes.

And the girl says to her dad, "Who was that marvelous stranger that saved my life?"

And her dad says, "I don't guess we'll ever know that now, honey."

We wrote seven or eight chapters on our book, all

ending up that way. After Ralph saved a lot of people in and out of the water—girls, usually, and once a puppy—he does a vanishing act every time because, see, he's got to go it alone to keep free.

The problem with that book, which we called *RALPH, THE FREE*, was that we began to believe it. We were always believing things just because we wanted to believe them. It was a habit that lingered on a lot longer—two years anyway.

Maybe we thought the real Ralph was holding out on us, so we had to create another Ralph to make up for it. Of course, it never crossed our minds that the real Ralph was teaching two grade school kids strictly for the salary involved. You don't think like that in the fifth grade. You don't want to.

We even seriously discussed the idea of presenting Ralph with a hand-recopied edition of *RALPH, THE FREE* as a token of friendship. But since he never said anything to us but "keep your head down," and "kick out of the water," and "only one of you on the board at a time," and like that, we decided we'd better not.

But the urge grew that summer to get through to the real Ralph. We figured if we said the right thing —the magic word or something—he'd become our friend. I see now we wanted to *be* him. I see now too that it was something like the way Elvan wanted to get through to us, but I didn't see that in time.

So on the tenth lesson—when Flip and I were about as good a pair of swimmers as Ralph could make us, we both realized that this was our last chance. To get through to him. We were pretty depressed. Not only was school about to start again, but Ralph was about to disappear from our lives.

On the last lesson, he put us through everything

we'd learned, and supervised without even getting into the pool himself. By then, he knew we could save ourselves if need be. It was a short lesson. Or maybe it seemed short because we wanted it to last. Always before, when the lesson was over, Ralph would send us off to the showers and stay in the pool for a solitary swim. On the last day, though, he was anxious to leave early himself.

So we all three turned up in the big shower room together. This was our one last chance. Flip and I were on one side—lathered up with Lava soap—and Ralph was under a spigot on the other side—minding his own business. I had the discouraging feeling that not only was he not sorry the lessons were over, but that he didn't even notice we were there.

Flip—who was only about four-foot-eleven at the time—was soaping up slowly—and thinking. Well ahead of time, I knew he was going to come up with something to say to Ralph—silent Ralph, Ralph, the Free—something that would leave a big impression on him. And then he said it.

Flip was a soprano at the time, and I can still hear how his voice rang out on those tile walls. "Hey, Ralph!" This made Ralph jump a little and turn around. "Listen, Ralph, me and Bry, we were wondering something." That put both Ralph and me on our guard. "What me and Bry were wondering is— when do you suppose we'll be getting hair on us like you got all down your front?"

Ralph's mouth kind of fell open. And while this question was still bouncing around the room, Ralph swallowed hard, and his face turned pink. He actually pulled his arms around the front of him to cover himself up. Then he whirled around, facing the wall. He jammed the faucets off and was out of that shower room in a flash. No slow and easy catlike movement like Ralph the Free.

So we were alone in there, with the Lava soap running off us in pink rivers. And the crazy part was, the tears started down my face, so I backed in under the shower head to hide them. Finally, I said, "Well, you've done it. You ran him off, and that's the last he'll ever have to do with us." It was too.

"What'd I say?" Flip said, bewildered. But he knew he'd scared our hero off for good.

We talked it over between ourselves later. Like why Flip's comment had had this electrifying effect on Ralph. I happened to remember that once my mom had said it was bad etiquette to make personal remarks in conversation. But that didn't seem to make much sense because most remarks are personal, including everything my mom ever says. Besides, we didn't figure Ralph was too involved with etiquette or anything like that.

"Maybe he thought it had something to do with sex," Flip said. But then we didn't see why Ralph, the big hero of all our adventures, would be shy on that subject.

Later that summer, we saw him again. He was riding down East Lincoln Avenue in a four-door Dodge. And a girl was driving. That was really the end of him as far as we were concerned.

Anyway, that's how we learned to swim, two years before the end of the friendship between Flip and me.

Twelve

"GOD ALMIGHTY, IT'S A COBRA!" Flip yelled and fell back flat on the mud bank. I was halfway up a convenient tree before the words were out of his mouth. We were both so scared we didn't know whether we were in India or down along Warnicke's Creek.

And it wasn't a cobra. It was a puff adder—what my dad calls a "hognose." When we came across it, our faces were about a foot and a half straight over the snake, which was puffing up fast and thinking seriously about going into a coil.

I hate a snake worse than anything. While Flip

was pulling himself together and darting around for a long branch to pester the puff adder with, I was yelling out instructions from my tree to get a big rock to drop on its head. But Flip was conquering his shock by trying to see how close he could get to the snake. By now, it was going into its second act.

When they get excited, puff adders swell up around the neck and look even uglier than they usually are. They may even start striking, pretending to be poisonous, which they aren't. But if they sense this isn't convincing anybody, they roll over and play dead. They're big fakers and harmless, but they can scare you to death.

As the old saying goes, snakes will leave you alone if you'll leave them alone. But we met up with this one purely by accident. It was the middle of that summer after seventh grade. We were down exploring along Warnicke's Creek a little way above the big railroad bridge. It's complete wilderness along there, and we were slogging through the undergrowth when we came on this old rowboat about halfway out of the water.

It wasn't anything but a wreck, but Flip thought maybe if we pushed it into the creek, it might float. Then we could continue exploring by water. We hadn't thought about details like oars, of course. We got behind the boat and started trying to push it down into the creek. It was dried hard to the bank, so we gave it a couple of kicks before it budged. Then it began to slip a little, and we were bent double giving it an almighty shoulder shove.

Suddenly, it shot right down into the water—and sank. And we were staring straight at the snout of the puff adder lying under it. It's a miracle we didn't sprawl right on it. There it was stretched out in a cool, damp, sunken part of the bank. The next thing I remember, I was up a tree and looking down.

While Flip thrashed around, looking for a long stick, the puff adder rolled over on its back, turning up a cream-colored belly. It was playing dead. I couldn't take my eyes off it. Then it changed its mind, and rolled back, and started oozing toward the weeds. I kept quiet, hoping it would get away before Flip came back. But he came charging up, swinging a big stick. And the snake stopped—"dead."

"Come on, move, you big con artist," Flip said, dancing around at a safe distance and poking at it with the stick. But it didn't quiver a scale.

"It's alive," I advised Flip from my tree.

"I know it," he said, and slid the stick under its body at the thick middle part. He lifted it up off the ground, and the big monster just hung there, limp as a dishrag.

"Throw that damn thing in the creek!" I yelled down, but Flip was acting cute now, so the show had to go on. For one thrilling flash, he hauled off like he was going to give it a pitch up on my branch. But instead, he let it slide down off the stick. It just lay there in a big S on the patch of pale grass where the rowboat had been.

He watched it for a minute, then threw the stick down and picked up a rock—about twice the size of a softball—and dropped it on the snake's head. Its body lashed once, looping off the ground. After that, it was still. And the rock, which was smooth, rolled down into the water. "It's not dead," I heard Flip say, low. There was a dent in the snake's head, and its neck was puffed about halfway out. Flip sidestepped it and retrieved the rock from the water. He dropped it on the snake's head again.

There was a lot of blood that time. It looked black from where I was. I said, "Don't. Let it go." But only to myself. Anyway, it was too late. The rock stayed on the snake's head. Its big body was rippling again, but, of course, that could mean it was dead for sure. They jump around a lot after death. Till sundown, some people say. I felt kind of dizzy and got a good hold on the trunk of my tree. It was okay to come down, but I hung on up there.

Later, when we were farther downstream, hacking our way through the vegetation, Flip said, "He might not have been dead." Dead or alive, it didn't make much difference to me. Snakes scare the devil out of me either way. I was ready to change the subject since I was so busy watching out for what might be coiled on the ground or draped over a low branch that the day was about shot for me anyway. But it was on Flip's mind. He really hated unfinished business.

Finally, I said to him, "Look, we'll go back later and see. If it's dead, it'll still be there. If it isn't, it'll be gone." But I was privately hoping Flip would forget the whole thing.

We were right under the railroad bridge then, which is like being in kind of a big, natural cathedral. Only it's higher than any church I've ever been in. It has three tall stone arches, and Warnicke's Creek runs through the center one. The bridge looks like one of those ancient Roman aqueducts. Even more so because now it's abandoned, and the railroad doesn't run trains over it any more. It's like a big ruin that's being reclaimed by nature.

We were probably the last generation to hear about the boy who fell off it. It was way back in the days of fast passenger service. This kid accepted a dare to walk across the bridge, which is strictly forbidden by the railroad. Anyway, he was right over the center arch when the train came—full steam ahead, so he couldn't outrun it. And since it's a single track bridge, this kid only had one chance. And that was to hang over the side till the train passed. He couldn't drop into the creek because it's too shallow —and a long drop. So he heaved himself down and swung over the side as the St. Louis train came whooshing by.

He nearly made it. But the vibrations must have got to him because he lost his grip, and fell into the creek, and split his skull. They fished his body out way downstream where it was snagged on a willow hanging down in the water. It's one of the local tales.

So we took a breather and looked straight up at the underside of the bridge and wondered about what that kid must have been thinking on the way down, if he had time to have any last thoughts. And this took our minds off the puff adder.

The reason we were out there was that we were in the last gasp of our local history study. It was the middle of the summer, and we were pretty bored. Nothing that used to be fun seemed like fun anymore. And it was kind of a strain trying not to think about Elvan Helligrew. And things were pretty quiet generally. The dead man business was ancient history by then.

So Flip took one last look through Estella Winkler Bates, which he'd illegally kept out of the library over the vacation. In an early chapter we'd overlooked because it didn't have any pictures, Estella told about how the first people in the area, not counting Indians, were a family called Warnicke, who'd built a cabin on the east bank of the creek in 1824. They planned to put in a sawmill on the creek and an inn. They were hoping that the stage coach would stop off there. But nothing came of it. The creek flooded every spring, so they didn't get their sawmill built, either that, or it washed away. And the stage crossed the creek a couple of miles above them where the ground was flatter. So the Warnickes just moved on farther west, Estella thought. Though she said there were some stories that the Indians got them. Anyway, the Warnickes were sort of losers, even though they were the original settlers.

According to the book, if you looked in the right place, you could still make out the foundation of the Warnicke's cabin and their stone fireplace, as of 1929. Flip thought if we went out there and explored, we might be able to find it again. Then maybe the newspaper would run a local-color story on it—and us, of course. I guess it continually ate at Flip that we carried the paper every evening without being in it, except for that one time.

So on the hottest day of the summer, we headed out to Warnicke's Creek by following the tracks, which is the easiest way to get there. We walked the rails until the hot steel blazed up through our sneaker soles. Then we stumped along on every fourth tie, which is just as hard going. It's a couple of miles out there at least. Past the park, through the edge of Beechurst Heights, then some farmland waiting to be subdivided, then a stinking part past the sewage treatment plant. After that, the track cuts through a high hill, and you come to the bridge across the creek valley and a large, faded-out, wooden signboard that ays:

CCESS TO THIS BRIDGE IS NOT ONLY DANGEROUS
T ILLEGAL. ENTRANCE UPON THIS RIGHT OF

WAY IS FORBIDDEN TO ALL BUT AUTHORIZED RAIL-
ROAD MAINTENANCE PERSONNEL. POSITIVELY NO
TRESPASSING BY ORDER OF

ST. LOUIS, EFFINGHAM & TERRE HAUTE RAILROAD

"We Opened the West"

So when we came to this sign, we skittered and
slid down the gravel bank and a steep dropoff until
we were down level with the creek. We'd been on
the lookout for the Warnickes' cabin remains for an
hour or so before we and the puff adder found each
other.

Even though it was cooler down there in the creek
bottom, we were working up a sweat trying to find
the Warnickes' traces. After the snake bit, I was getting less interested every minute. It wasn't much past
noon, and we hadn't got farther than maybe a hundred yards south of the bridge. We came out on a
wide spot in the creek—muddy, but it looked deep
enough for a swim. So we had the same idea at the
same time. Snakes or no snakes, we were ready for
a dip.

We weren't the Tom Sawyer types. Most of our
swimming had been in the Y pool back in the Ralph
Harvey days. But we were out of our T-shirts, Levis,
and underpants in a flash. Flip waded right in. I let
him get in butt-deep before I got my feet wet because
the water was light brown, and you couldn't see
where where you were stepping.

I was just starting in when he disappeared completely. But he bobbed back up like a cork with his
hair matted down all over his face, sputtering and
spitting. "Damn slimy dropoff," he said. "Start swimming." So we eased off, dog-paddling and trying

to keep our chins out of the water, which was probably polluted. It was lukewarm too, but we horsed around in it awhile, and he tried to duck me, but my arms were longer so I could keep him off. Then we got out and remembered we didn't have any towels. So we flopped down in the long grass—after I made a careful check for reptiles.

We talked about this and that. Like what we ought to have brought for lunch, except we'd started out so soon after breakfast that we hadn't been hungry then and didn't think ahead. Then we talked about how big Arlene DeSappio's knockers were and wondered if she was still growing. Then we got a little sleepy, and I'd have drifted off except I still had snakes on the brain.

But Flip gave me a jolt by saying, "Doesn't look like we're catching up with Ralph Harvey, does it?"

This came as a slight shock since neither one of us had mentioned Ralph for two years. But I knew what he meant. I was getting a wisp or two of hair in my armpits and beginning to use spray deodorant when I thought of it. And I had some hair coming in down below too, but nothing to speak of. Flip was still slick as a whistle. I didn't know whether what he said was embarrassing or not. I decided it wasn't, seeing as how Flip said it, and we were alone. "Yeah, well," I said, "who wants to look like an ape?"

"Yeah, who?" Flip said. After a slight pause.

He had his head propped up against a tree root, looking back in the direction of the bridge. And I was headed the other way. Pretty soon, he gave a little jump, and then he was up on his feet in a crouch, squinting off in the distance.

"By God, there's somebody up on the bridge," he said. I looked around and, sure enough, way off in the

110

distance, there was somebody standing up there, right in the middle, directly over the creek. Facing toward us.

It was weird. Way out there away from everything. For a second, I had a feeling whoever was up there was about to jump. But he didn't. He just stood up there, silhouetted against the blue sky—like a trapeze artist.

"It's a tramp," I said, quiet, because your voice carries out in the open like that. And it scared me. We both started pulling on our clothes. When we were dressed, whoever it was on the bridge had walked a few paces in the direction of town and was sitting down with his legs hanging over the side.

I don't know why it scared me. Just that it was somebody up there, watching us maybe. And our being naked and all. I wanted to head off downstream, away from the bridge, and maybe come out on the route and walk back home that way. I wanted to put some distance between us and the bridge. I don't know now if I remembered about the dead man in the woods being a tramp or not. I don't think so, but I was tense anyway.

But Flip was heading back toward the bridge, keeping close to the trees. He looked back once and motioned for me to follow. It was his I've-got-a-plan gesture. And like a sheep, I followed him. Like a dumb sheep.

Cutting along in a straight line, we were back by the bridge before I knew it. There was open territory just before you get to the bottom of the arches. And Flip shot across it and under the bridge. I realized that if the tramp was still up on the bridge, he could look straight down as we crossed under him. Maybe he could have been watching us all the way up from the swimming place. I couldn't tell for sure. But I felt his eyes burning into the top of my head as I broke cover and made a dash under the bridge.

"He's still up there," Flip whispered when I came up next to him. "I looked up and saw his feet."

"What are we doing?" I whispered.

"Be quiet and keep up with me," he muttered. Then he headed on, still staying next to the creek. I had to stay right on his heels to keep the branches from whipping back and cutting me across the face. We were moving so fast I couldn't think about where we were going. I was wondering if the tramp had got up and turned around and might be watching us from this side of the bridge. I didn't look to see, though.

So we were right back by the scuttled rowboat and the puff adder before I knew where I was. The snake was still there, and I threw on my brakes before I got up to it. Flip circled in on it and grabbed it by the tail. My knees nearly gave out on me. I wanted to beg him to leave it alone. But he'd already jerked it so that its squashed head flipped out from under the rock. It was the deadest snake you ever saw. And I was the scaredest kid.

"Come on," Flip said, like I was supposed to know what he had in mind. "We'll head up this side of the hill and come out right over the railroad cut. Maybe we'll get there before he comes on down the track." Then Flip started scrambling up the hill, dragging the dead puff adder behind him.

I stood there, mad, with tears in my eyes. Flip turned around and said, "Come on!" in a hoarse whisper. So I did. At a distance. It was a tough climb. I kept Flip in sight ahead and above me, with the bloody-headed snake bobbing along behind him. It must have been about three feet long because its head grazed the ground. At some places, if he'd turned loose of it, it would have dropped back on me. And why the thought of this didn't stop me cold, I don't know. I was just running and climbing because he was.

We were out of the trees and up in the high grass on top of the hill. Behind us, you could see a section of the tracks crossing the bridge, wavering in the sun and heat. Flip was running in a low crouch right up to the cut where the man-made cliff face dropped straight down to the tracks. He flopped down in the weeds and crawled up to the edge. I dropped down too, but circled way around to one side of him because I knew he was dragging that damned snake through the grass, and I didn't want to come up on it all of a sudden.

So I got up to the edge of the cut a few feet nearer the bridge than he was. The sun was getting over in the west by then so I was about half-blinded by it. I had to squint to see if somebody was walking along the tracks. But I had to look all the way back to the bridge before I saw him. He was just getting up from where he'd been sitting. He was coming our way. Just a shape in the distance, dark, with a halo of light around him.

"He's headed this way," I said.

"Right." Flip was rustling around in the grass, doing something with the snake.

I could just see this shape way off and thought it was funny he wasn't carrying anything. I knew tramps didn't carry all their gear in a red bandanna on the end of a stick in real life. But I had seen a couple before—live ones, I mean. And sometimes they had

113

old beat-up cardboard suitcases. But this one was just walking along, slow, with his arms free—a big guy. I inched back from the edge of the cliff.

I had time then to realize what we were doing. Or rather, what Flip was about to do. Throw the dead snake down on the tramp and scare the wits out of him. Or maybe, throw it down right in front of him. Then a funny thing happened to me. A couple of things. It was like that dream I'd had. The one where I was dreaming I was walking along with Flip but I was somewhere else at the same time—standing way off, watching. It felt like a dream too. The sun dazzling everything, making the whole world either pure light or black shadows. It was like I was the tramp, walking along down there, maybe knowing we were up above, maybe not. But I was walking along the track instead of the tramp, feeling the rocks through the holes in my shoes. I was the tramp and I was about to get a dead snake dropped on my shoulders—if Flip's aim was any good. I could feel the snake hit me and the black spatters of snake's blood on me.

And for the first time in my life, I thought something Flip had thought up was senseless. Not just not worth doing. Senseless. I was going to tell him not to do it, tell him he wasn't going to do it. But I couldn't take my eyes off the tramp, who was getting bigger and closer. So I put my head down in the grass and counted up to ten, which would bring the tramp ten paces closer. Then I was going to get up and stop Flip, who I could hear breathing.

But when I looked up, and then over the cliff, and then down at an angle, the sun wasn't in my eyes anymore. And I was looking down at Elvan Helligrew. And he was looking up at me.

I stood up, and Elvan stopped. I thought for a

minute he was going to turn back. But it was too late. I was pretty sure I could read his mind. That he was remembering our dire warning about not following us around. That he was pretending he hadn't really followed us out there and spied on us all he could. And maybe how he'd even let us see him on the bridge to show us how brave he was.

But Flip whispered, "Get your damn head down."

"It's Elvan," I said. "It's him down there."

Flip poked his head out of the weeds to make sure. "For Chrissakes," he said, "that's better yet." He rustled around, getting ready to let fly with the snake.

"No," I said and walked over to him. He had the snake all lined up with the edge of the dropoff, ready to grab it and drop it. "We're not going to do it," I said to him, loud.

"Maybe you're not, but I am."

Elvan had stopped walking, so there was no big hurry. But Flip grabbed the snake just under the neck. And I stepped up and put my foot on his hand that was holding it. I was free of my snake phobia for the time being. And Flip looked up at me, more surprised than I'd ever seen him.

"No, you're not," I said. And I don't think he even heard the shake in my voice. His hand opened out, even though I wasn't putting much weight on it. He moved it away from under my sneaker, and he never took his eyes off my face.

Now—two years later—I can see the advantage I had right then. I can see what I might have been able to do with it. I might have been able to change things for all of us, for Elvan too. But I didn't see it then. I wasn't really ready to stop being a follower. Not yet.

Flip stood up, and I kicked the snake back into the

tall grass without looking at it. My foot tingled where my shoe touched the snake.

All this time, Elvan must have been standing down there wondering what in the hell was going on. But I turned away and walked up over the crown of the hill. I was shaking—maybe because of the snake. And I decided I'd walk a long way home, through some pastures away from the tracks. I didn't care if Flip came along or not.

He did. We were over a woven-wire fence and walking along through a field spattered with cow pies when he finally said, "I don't think we'd have done it."

"You'd have done it, all right. Without thinking."

"Yeah, I would have," he said after a few more steps. "It'd of been a dumb-ass thing to do. You were right. This time."

Thirteen

Summer was slipping away, and I'd been nagging my dad, when he was home, to take me on the truck with him. By August, he was still holding out, but getting quieter about it. Since he's generally pretty quiet anyway, it took me awhile to realize he was getting even quieter. So I kept at him every chance I got, especially when Mom wasn't around.

Finally, he gave in and said he'd take me on an overnight down to Memphis and back, but he couldn't see why I wanted to go. He'd rather stay home if somebody gave him the choice.

When my mom got wind of it, she carried on awhile till Dad finally told her, "I give him my word, and that's that."

I'd wanted to have Flip along too, but I knew that wasn't in the cards. With Dad, and the relief driver, and me, it was a full cab. As it was, one of us had to lie up in the bunk behind the seat while the other one rode next to the driver.

Flip and I had gotten over the snake business without going over it. It made a difference with us for awhile. We were a little bit more polite with each other. More careful with each other, anyway. So when I found out I was going to get to make the Memphis run, I told Flip I wished he was coming too. Since it meant he'd have to carry the route alone for a couple of evenings, I had to say something.

The afternoon we left I was pretty worked up, but I played it very low key around Mom. She was saying things like, "I don't want you sitting up all night. You sleep in the bunk." And, "I don't want you eating that slop in those all-night truck stops. And no coffee." And, "Don't sit on the toilet seats in those places. You don't know what you could pick up." Talk about personal comments.

We got out on the road about sundown. It was Interstate 57, that cuts straight down the state to the bridge at Cairo. Pete Langbecker was relief driver, and he started out in the bunk. I guess he went to sleep right away; he's even quieter than Dad so you can't always tell when he's awake. Technically, Dad's his boss, but they're buddies and play pinochle at the Elks whenever they're both home. It's a close friendship, I guess, even if they don't talk much to each other. Maybe *because* they don't talk much.

I started out sitting by Dad, and you're way up

above the other traffic. Perched up that high you can see straight ahead over every car on the road. And you can spot trouble a mile off. It was hot even after sundown, but there was a wind. Hot and steady, coming out of the south to meet us. "I'll be in ninth the whole way if that wind holds," Dad said. He was talking about gears.

"What are we carrying?" I asked him.

He couldn't remember. Truckers don't do the loading anymore. So he told me to look at the manifest. It said we were carrying a load of knocked-down insulated fiberboard cartons for large kitchen appliances.

"Is that a good load to haul?"

"Everything's about the same," he said, "except heavy machinery than can shift on you."

It's funny about driving along at night. There's all that time to talk, and you can't think of too much to say. It'd always been so easy to think of things to talk about with Flip. But I was beginning to want something else.

South of Centralia, you start seeing the oil wells pumping out in the fields. They look like squatty, little dinosaurs with their heads moving up and down in a steady motion. We were rolling along at seventy, but, once in a while, a car would pass us. If it dimmed its lights as it came around us, Dad would dim his. Then after they'd get past, some of them would hit their dimmers again as kind of a salute.

We had the windows down, and there was a strong smell of diesel fuel. But over it, you could smell open country. Ragweed, and dust, and an occasional whiff of barnyard. I was trying hard to stay awake and wondering when we'd switch off so I'd get the bunk. I thought maybe if I closed my eyes but stayed sitting straight up, Dad wouldn't notice I was napping.

He didn't, I guess, because after awhile he cleared his throat like he was about to say something. Since he doesn't talk all the time, you can usually tell when he's getting ready. So I popped my eyes open. He eased forward from the seat and worked his shoulders around to loosen them up. I was still waiting.

"Your mother ever talk to you about things?" he said after awhile, never taking his eyes off the road.

"What things?"

"Oh—you know—about how you ought to act."

"Manners?"

"No, not manners. I know she talks a lot of manners. She talks them to me."

"Well, what then?" (I knew what then.)

"About how you ought to act to keep out of trouble. With girls."

I sat there awhile without saying anything, but I knew I had to say something because I couldn't let it pass. I wondered, too, if Pete was awake behind us, but decided it didn't matter.

"I don't think she thinks I'm old enough yet to be fooling around with girls."

"You're getting there," Dad said. Then after another mile or so, "Anything you don't know you want to know?"

"I guess not."

"You sure?"

Actually, I couldn't be a hundred per cent sure. But I started to say I was. Instead, I said, "If there ever is anything I don't hear on my own, I'll ask you."

"I hope I'll know," Dad said.

South of Marion, he geared down and eased over toward the pull-off road. We were coming up on a cluster of lights and a giant electric sign—of a smiling chef swinging a big arm—with neon tubing on it. Underneath, it said:

SWEET SINGER OF THE SOUTHLAND
EAT ALL NIGHT
SHOWERS AND BUNKS
RATES FOR TRUCKERS
DIXIE BEGINS HERE

We pulled up in a long line of semis and livestock trucks full of cattle. When Dad cut the motor, the silence was deafening, even with the cows bawling all around us. They say the steady whine of a big diesel motor can rob you of your hearing permanently. I wondered if it could happen to Dad. He poked Pete, who rolled right down out of the bunk as we were climbing out of the cab.

It was after midnight, but, inside SWEET SINGER OF THE SOUTHLAND, it was like high noon on a busy day. There was a long counter lined with truckers eating full meals. And maybe a hundred tables, mostly crowded. And flypaper hanging down from the ceiling. A loudspeaker system was blaring country music. And the whole place smelled like deep-fried everything. We found three stools together, and I had what Dad and Pete had: chicken-fried steak and cottage fries, tossed salad with blue cheese dressing, two cloverleaf rolls, apple pie with cheese, and coffee. And I could have eaten that much again.

Our waitress was named Rosalee. It said so on her name tag. She came right over as soon as we sat down and said, "Here's the Dunthorpe boys!" Then she gave me a look, and turned to Dad, and back at me again. "Now I know who this is," she said, right at

121

me. "Don't tell me now. I've got it—Brian. Right?" This came as a big surprise to me. How this Rosalee, who was young and medium pretty, knew who I was. "Oh your daddy talks about you," she said. "I knew you quick as you walked in. They going to make a trucker out of you, honey?"

"What's good tonight, Rosalee?" Dad said. I think he was a little embarrassed.

"Everything," she said. "But some of it's better than the rest of it, and we're out on the catfish."

"I wouldn't eat catfish if you tore up the check," Dad said. And Pete snorted.

"I know it," Rosalee said. "You don't eat nothing but steak, so why ask?" But she gave him a big smile and winked at Pete, who ducked his head down.

After that, it was my turn in the bunk, but Dad stayed at the wheel. He'd rather do all the night driving and let Pete drive back in daylight. And the minute I stretched out in the bunk, I was wide-awake. Probably because I was swelled up with all that food. So I poked at the pillow and watched the road over Dad's shoulder and all the little pinpoint lights on the dash.

That late, the traffic was thinned out, mostly trucks. But suddenly a minibus, with a home-done, bright purple paint job, rocked around us. Dad must have seen it coming up on us in the rear view mirror. It went by so close it nearly sliced the mirror off us and zoomed past like we were standing still. "Sonofabitch," Pete said. It lost a little speed ahead of us because we were on a grade. It was weaving and straddling the line between our lane and the pass lane.

"Bunch of idiots," Dad said, and gave them a blast on the air horn. But over the crest of the hill, they pulled away from us and out of the range of our lights. They had to be doing ninety.

Then we were alone on the road for maybe half an hour. And I must have started to doze off because I jumped when Dad started pumping on the brakes and the truck began to pull back. Way up ahead, we could see something off on the shoulder of the road. Dad saw it first. It was the square back of the minibus, but it looked different. Then we could see why. It was the rear end of it, but it was upside down. Flipped. Dad kept working the brakes, and we were pulling up to it, off on the shoulder, which was flat gravel. When he stopped, our lights flooded the whole scene—the overturned bus and the broken glass glittering like rock salt all around it. And the upended wheels still turning. But not a sign of life.

Pete was fishing around in the box under the seat for flares. I started to follow Dad when he ran up toward the wreck, but he told me to cut on back and help Pete plant a flare behind us. It didn't dawn on me at the time that Pete wouldn't need any help with that. And when I got way up the road behind with him, I thought maybe I didn't want to go back to see what had happened. Pete did, though. And we loped back.

Dad had the door on the driver's side open. "Go on back and get the big flashlight," he said to me instead of to Pete, who'd know where it was.

"God, that's awful," I heard Pete say when I came back with the flashlight.

"You go on back in the cab," Dad said to me. He must have known I wouldn't do it. When I handed him the flashlight, I tried not to look in the minibus, but I couldn't keep from it.

The driver was wedged in between the steering column and the front window, which was cracked into a big star and bulging out. There's no hood on a minibus, so his body was almost pushed out onto the gravel. Dad went around the door and started kicking at the big wedges of glass. The driver finally fell out onto the ground. Dad stooped down over him, and Pete held the flashlight low to the ground. They were in a tight huddle, and as long as I was pretty sure I couldn't see much, I tried to see a little. "He's gone," I heard Pete say. And they stood up at the same time.

We could hear another truck coming upon us from behind, gearing down as he saw the flare. It pulled up next to us, and the relief driver on our side stuck his head out. "You want us here or shall we go on and send back the troopers from Shawnee Villa?"

"Hold it a minute," Dad said and turned back to the bus. It takes awhile to tell it, but this all happened fast. Dad moved like he was only a step away from everything. He played the light across the upside-down front seat, and there was a girl there. She had on a shoulder strap safety belt, and she was hanging with her head down. "Hold it a minute," Dad yelled again. He and Pete ran around the front, skirting the body of the driver.

They had a job to get the door on the far side wrenched open. They both reached in and had to work without seeing. Trying to get her safety belt off her and lift her out.

They carried her back behind the bus, full into the beam from our headlights. She had long, smooth, blond hair that swung under her. Dad had her under the arms, and Pete had hold of her under her knees. They laid her down gently, away from the broken glass of the rear window.

She was wearing stretch slacks and a yellow blouse tied in a knot in front so her bare midriff and belly-button showed. There was a line of red on her forehead, but nothing else. She looked asleep. Dad took her wrist. It flopped like a doll's. There was a long moment then. We all waited and the relief driver on the other truck held his door open, but didn't get out.

"She's gone too," Dad said. But he was looking down at her like he couldn't believe it. She still just looked asleep. I walked right over to her. Her eyes weren't quite closed. And she had on dark lipstick that made her mouth look purple. She just looked—relaxed. Like she might stir in her sleep. Dad put her arm down on the ground. Then he turned away from me and walked over to the rig that was idling in the right lane. "There's two of them. Send the troopers back and the ambulance, but you can tell them it's too late."

When we were alone, Pete planted another flare at the edge of the road. He and Dad went through the back of the minibus, looking for something to cover up the bodies with. There was a tangle of stuff back there. I could see some of it from the red light of the flare. A big guitar, for one thing, and some books. It was stuff that had just been thrown in the back end, so it was all in a mess. They found a couple of sleeping bags, but no blankets. So they pulled them out and put one over the driver and the other one over the girl.

The wind had died down, and it was hotter than ever. But the stars were out—bright like they are in the country. They seemed cold.

It wasn't too long before we saw the revolving red lights coming up ahead of us. A regular state police sedan and an International Harvester ambulance behind it. They U-ed in across the center strip and pulled off in front of the minibus.

Right away, they radioed back for a wrecker and checked the bodies, moving like Dad—quick, but easy. And they discovered that the right front tire was blown out. All four tires were about bald.

It wasn't too long before we were on the road again. Away from the red flares, it was dark—almost like none of it had ever happened. Pete was dozing in his seat, but I was wide-awake again in the bunk.

I couldn't get the picture of the dead girl out of my mind—the red line on her forehead and the peaceful look on her face. Dad was thinking too.

"They were asking for it, driving at all on slick rubber.

"I've seen my share of pileups. You don't get hardened to them."

I figured he was thinking specifically about the girl too.

I remembered what Mrs. Garrison said that time she gave Flip and me the Kennedy half dollars. That we'd be better men for having seen death. Then, we thought she might be cracked. But maybe she was talking about men like Dad.

I wondered, for a minute, if this girl would come back in my dreams like old Gold Tooth had. I didn't worry about it much, though. For one thing, I felt like maybe I'd never go sound asleep again. But even if I did dream about her, it would be different. If she ever came back to me, she'd come back alive.

But something else in my mind was trying to connect up those two deaths. Like maybe how frustrated Flip would be if he'd been along to see this accident —with no mystery about it. No clues to follow up.

Just a quick crunch on an open highway No loose ends, except maybe insurance.

And it was funny how the girl who didn't even look dead seemed more dead than the man in the woods, who'd been long gone. Maybe that's the way it is in Asia and places like that—death all around you and as natural as living. I read one time how, in Calcutta, there's a patrol that goes around every morning collecting the bodies of people who starved to death in the streets overnight. Like garbage.

It dawned on me then about just how much Flip and I had really enjoyed the whole thing. It made me feel like we'd been a couple of creeps. As creepy as Elvan.

Fall

Fourteen

On warm days in September the high school
  band
Is up with the birds and marches along our street,
Boom boom,
To a field where it goes boom boom until eight
  forty-five
When it marches, as in the old rhyme, back,
  boom boom,
To its study halls, leaving our street
Empty except for the leaves that descend, to no
  drum,

And lie still.
In September
A great many high school bands beat a great many drums,
And the silences after their partings are very deep.

That's the poem I'd recited for Miss Klimer's benefit back in the spring of seventh grade. She went for it because it was about real life and had sound effects. But it's more of an autumn-type poem. And even though we were only starting the eighth grade and not high school, I always connect it with that fall. When I think about that fall.

The town was warm and empty, and it was like having to go back to school in the middle of the summer. It always starts too soon.

Eighth grade didn't show much promise of being any different from seventh. Not like starting in the high school, which was still a year off. Coolidge Middle School—what was once called Coolidge Junior High—tries hard to keep up with the times. They call English class "Language Arts" and the Library's officially known as "The Resource Materials Center." They have a lot of progressive ideas, but the place is full of old-time relics. Half the rooms still have lift-top desks bolted to the floor. And inkwells.

Everybody with last names starting with A through C was in the same homeroom—from Loretta Armbruster to Clarence Cochran. I was right there in the middle. And, of course, Flip, being a T, was in another homeroom. So we didn't get together until the real classes started for the day.

What you didn't want to keep locked up safe in

your locker, you kept in your homeroom desk. Non-essentials. It was one morning about the third week of school when I reached in my desk for my notebook and pulled out a little package instead. All neatly wrapped up in brown paper and twine. No name on it or anything. There was just time to get it open—with Mary Beth Borden snooping over my shoulder to see what it was all about.

Inside the wrappings was a little box, jewelry store sized. I could feel Mary Beth's hot breath on my neck as I opened it up. First, there was a layer of cotton. Then a folded-up note, which I transferred to my shirt pocket as it was—to Mary Beth's disappointment. Then another layer of cotton. And in the bottom was a medal. I pulled it out. It was a ribbon-covered bar. Hanging down from it was a gray part like a coin. Very familiar. Like the knife at the bridge. The same laurel leaf wreath circled around a very authentic swastika. "Here we go again," I said, but not to Mary Beth.

The first class was Social Problems. We sat in a friendly circle in there, but with assigned seats. Flip's was directly across from me. There wasn't time for any real communication, but he looked right at me, nodded, and tapped his chest. I got the message. He'd received a medal too, which was no surprise. Then I remembered the note, and as I pulled it out of my pocket, I saw that Flip kept staring at me, waiting for me to read it if I hadn't already.

Elvan had decided to disguise his handwriting, which was pretty pointless, but I guess he thought it helped build up the mystery a little. The only thing it did was make it hard to read. But Elvan didn't want too much mystery:

FOR SOMEONE WHO FOUND THE DEAD MAN IN
THE WOODS LAST SPRING *ATTENTION*

You will find out some more interesting evidence
if you come to THE PLACE in the woods
where it happened. Be there this evening at 5:30
don't be late bring this medal to identify your-
selfs with

I crumpled it up and gave out a big disgusted sigh
for Flip's benefit. He just shook his head.

At lunch, we compared notes and medals. They
were pretty much the same. I was all for marching
right back to Elvan's table and dumping them in
front of him. "I told you it'd be like this," I said to
Flip. "We'll have him on our backs for years if we
don't stop him right now."

"I know it," he said. But that's all he said.

I started to get up then, but Flip grabbed hold of
my arm. "Sit down. Not now."

"Well, not at 5:30, either," I said to him. But I
might as well have saved my breath.

Because at quarter after five we were heading out
Jefferson Avenue with the main gates of Marquette
Park at the end of it. Flip had been too quiet while
we carried the route. Afterward, when he just turned
down Jefferson Avenue like it was understood between us that we were going to meet Elvan, I finally
got mad.

"Where do you think we're going?"

"To meet Elvan."

"I've got a better idea."

"What?" Flip said, like he didn't want to hear it.

"Let him stand out there waiting for us a few
hours. That'll cure him of planting anonymous notes."

"I doubt it," Flip said, and I guess I did too, but I didn't like to admit it.

"But, dammit, if we meet him out there according to *his* instructions, he'll feel more like Hitler than ever. I'm for not giving him the satisfaction."

"It's not for giving him any satisfaction," Flip said. "We're the ones going to get the satisfaction if anybody does."

"It'd satisfy me just fine to go home."

"So go."

I got as far as starting to turn off on the last cross street before the park gates. I was getting tired of playing by Flip's rules. But that wasn't so bad. I hated playing by Elvan's.

"But if we don't go," Flip said to my back, "we'll be making a mistake for two reasons." I stood there. He knew he had me. I knew he had me. "First, he'll just keep after us if we don't scare him off for good. And second, we won't be satisfied if we don't find out what he's got to say that he's so anxious to tell us."

That turned me around. "Look, Flip, you don't really think he has any evidence, do you? It's just something he's thought up to say. Right?"

"How do we know till we hear?"

"What we're going to hear from him is a bunch of bull. What I want to know from you right now is do you think Elvan killed the dead man?"

Flip just stood there, looking at me.

"Do you think he killed the dead man, and now he's decided to confess to us?" I said, loud.

"No," he said, finally. "No motive. And no guts."

"All right then, why play along with him?"

"I told you why," Flip said. "To scare him off. For good. We don't need him."

"Then let's get it over with," I said. And Flip

strolled off into the park like he didn't particularly care whether I came along or not.

"We'll play by your rules—one last time," I said. But maybe I didn't say it out loud.

Looking back, I think I knew right then that making the break with Elvan was going to break off the friendship between Flip and me too. I don't know. It's hard to tell about friendships. I haven't had a close one since. Maybe I only knew it later. But now, it seems right that I knew it when we walked through the park. That something was happening. Or something was over. Something that didn't have much to do with Elvan at all. Like from then on, Flip and I wouldn't have each other to lean on as usual. Like game time was over. For good.

The swans were two white blotches out on Dreamland Lake. They floated out there like plastic toys, hardly moving. And the other ducks were all clustered together next to the shore. It was as still as a picture. Or like one of those little scenes in a glass paperweight before you shake it up and the snow falls.

The sun was just setting behind the woods and shining through the trees and the fancy ironwork on the bridge over the lake. It all looked so normal that it seemed artificial.

We went into the tunnel of branches, moving like a couple of Indians. My heart was pounding, and that made me feel like a fool. I wanted to ask Flip if he thought Elvan was already there, but I didn't want to make a sound. We stopped when we got to the creek and looked across at the clearing. It looked empty. But then, it had looked empty the day we took the pictures too. I didn't give the dead man a thought. All I could think of was which tree Elvan might be back of.

Flip cleared the creek first. There weren't so many leaves on the ground. The trees hadn't even started to turn much yet. Instead of marching up to where the dead man had been, Flip settled down on the roller coaster block. The one with the swastika carved on it. He seemed cool, but he was looking around.

"Well, which tree is he behind this time?" I said, low.

"Who knows? Let him have his fun."

"Maybe we're early."

"We're about on time."

"Maybe he's not . . ."

"Shut up," Flip whispered. "Listen."

But there wasn't anything to hear but the breeze in the trees and a honk or two from the ducks.

We could see a little section of the shore path curving around from the far side of the lake. Just a narrow open place in the trees. We both watched it, even though he could have been coming up on us from any direction. It was a warm evening, and the lake smelled like the sewage treatment plant only milder.

Pretty soon, we saw him coming around the edge of the lake. He just took a couple of steps where we could watch him, but it was Elvan all right. Ambling along, taking his time. Maybe even stopping to have a look at the swans. Because it seemed like a long time before he battered through the trees on the other side of the clearing. He wasn't creeping this time.

"Hey, buddies," he said. And waved. He was wearing a pair of outsize corduroys. You could hear the little rasping sound they made on the insides of his legs when he walked straight across where the dead man had been. Toward us. "You bring the medals?" he said, walking up close.

"Yeah, we got them in our pockets, Elvan," Flip said, easing off the concrete block. "Want them?"

"No, that's okay," Elvan said. "You don't really need any identification."

Then he dried up—like he hadn't thought things out past that point. The three of us were just facing one another, toes almost touching. After awhile, Flip said, "What about this so-called evidence you've got up your sleeve, Elvan? Want to tell us about it?"

Elvan started kicking backward, digging his heel in the dirt. He looked nervous, playing it by ear. All I could think of was that it was boring. Standing around waiting for him to think up something to invent. He was a slow thinker.

"Yeah, well, you guys pretty much have the picture," he said, looking at the ground. "I mean you guys found the knife, so I guess you pretty much have the picture."

"What picture?" Flip said, standing up straight so he'd be as tall as Elvan.

"Well, I mean I could fill in some details. I mean if you want the details."

"Anything you want to tell us, Elvan."

"Well, here's the way it was. Like this. I was out here in the woods, doing some exploring, oh, sometime last winter. There was a lot of snow on the ground. I forget the day. And I had my knife with me in case I might need it. You buddies know the one I mean. And I was right here in the woods, back there in the open place. You know the place. Well, I heard something behind me. Something suspicious. I heard this footstep in the leaves right behind me, so I turned around quick. It was this tramp. A real mean-looking guy. Dangerous-looking with red eyes. And he started coming for me . . ."

Elvan was talking faster, and his face was lighting up like it did sometimes when he was really wound up. Once he got his story going, he was enjoying it, beginning to believe it himself.

". . . So I pulled out my knife and let him have a look at cold steel and . . ."

"Wait a minute, Elvan, hold on now," Flip said. "You mentioned snow on the ground, but then you said you heard the tramp's step in the leaves. That doesn't figure. I don't think we believe that, Elvan."

His face sagged. He swallowed and looked confused, just like he'd looked back in grade school if the teacher ever called on him. He thought a long time before he answered. You could see the wheels turning, very slow. "Yeah, well, there's leaves *under* the snow. There wasn't too much snow." Then instead of going on with the story, he just looked at Flip and me, like he wanted us to okay this part before he went on.

"Then what happened when the tramp saw cold steel, Elvan?"

"Well, he told me to hand over the knife and any money I had on me. He said he needed money for something to eat. He could tell it was a valuable weapon. The knife, I mean. It is."

"Sure, it is."

"Well, then he made a grab for my throat since he saw I wasn't going to give up my knife. I mean I was armed and I've studied combat warfare. Hand to hand fighting." He slowed down again then. Like he didn't exactly know how to handle the big moment in the story.

"What happened when he grabbed you by the neck, Elvan? What'd you do then?"

"Well, then I had my knife in my right hand, see? Down low. And I brought it up fast and jammed it into him. I mean it really happened fast. Self-defense."

"Where'd you jam it into him, Elvan?"

"Right over there," Elvan said, waving his arm backward. "Right where you guys found him."

"No, Elvan, I mean where in his *body* did you jam it?" Flip said, very patient-sounding.

"Oh, I see what you mean. Well . . . right into his . . . gut. Right into his big, soft gut."

He shut up then. And looked at Flip, then at me. His little eyes were as big as they could get. It was evening then, and his eyes looked black in his round face.

"That about it, Elvan?" Flip said. "That about all you have to tell us?"

"Yeah, well that's about all I can think—remember. I mean he was dead. No question about that. There was a lot of blood on the snow."

"And the leaves," Flip added.

"Yeah, on them too."

Flip zipped up his windbreaker and said to me, "Okay, Bry, it's getting late. Let's shove off." Like Elvan wasn't even there with us. I was ready to go. I started to reach in my pocket to give Elvan his medal back.

But when he saw we were about to pull out, he yelled out at us, "Hey, wait a minute!" For a second, his voice had that sound it had when we were at his house—commanding, sort of. "You guys wouldn't tell on a buddy, would you?"

140

And Flip turned around to him and said, "What's to tell, Elvan?"

Elvan opened his mouth, but nothing came out. Then his face collapsed. It looked too small for his body. But we waited, and so, finally, he said to me, "It's true. Every bit of it. You believe me, don't you, Brian?"

"No," I said.

But he was looking at Flip again. "I wouldn't lie to you guys. I wouldn't put you on." He grabbed Flip's arm. "You're my best buddies."

"Turn loose of my arm," Flip said.

"But . . ."

"Butt out, Elvan," Flip said. He wasn't talking loud, but there was hate in his voice—real hate. "Just how damn stupid you take us for? How long you think you can play us for a couple of suckers?"

It wasn't just what he said. He'd told Elvan off before. But it was the sound in his voice. It scared me as bad as it did Elvan. "Now I'm going to give you a count of three. And when I hit three, you'd better be out of sight. Because we've had about all your crazy-assed talk we can put up with. So let's just see how fast you can do a vanishing act because if you hang around here, you're going to be one sorry slob. One."

Elvan pulled back and stared at Flip. He must have forgotten how much he'd enjoyed talk like that before. He could tell this was different.

"Two."

Fifteen

Elvan lit out running. He didn't jump the creek. He waddled right down in it and up the other side, wet to his knees. His big legs were pumping away. He slipped once and came down hard on one knee, but he was up again, moving faster than he'd ever moved. He bobbed around a little, looking for the path out of the woods, the way we'd come in.

"Three," Flip yelled, loud enough for him to hear. "Come on, let's go after him."

"Let's go the other way."

"No, we'll just tail him till he hears us behind him. It'll keep him moving. Come on."

We jumped the creek together and kicked along the path, half running, making extra noise. But I think Elvan was too far ahead to hear. We loped along, bent over under the low branches, and came out into the open by the end of the lake.

Out of the corner of my eye, I saw the big swans cutting across over the water, working their wings, heading up toward the woodsy end. I couldn't see Elvan ahead of us, though. Not at first.

But I was looking straight up along the path, past the barricades at the approach to the bridge. Flip stopped dead. He threw out one arm and opened his mouth. Then I saw Elvan. He'd gone over the Park Department sawhorses that warn you off the bridge. And he was pounding over it. Almost at the top of the arch over the middle of the lake.

Flip cupped his hands over his mouth and yelled, "Elvan, stop!"

And Elvan did. He was just a shape on the bridge. Like he was miles away instead of yards. Like that day out at Warnicke's Creek.

"Elvan, watch what you're doing. The floor's rotted out!"

Flip was screaming it. So loud I couldn't even understand him. But I didn't need to. I knew how rotted out that floor was. Without even going past the barricades, you could see daylight through the cracks in it.

"Grab hold of the handrail," Flip yelled. "Hang on to that!"

Elvan had turned back toward us. Like he was listening—or trying to hear. But he didn't grab hold of the handrail. It was cast-iron, and he could work his way back to either end of the bridge if he'd just hang on and go hand over hand. But he just stayed there in the middle with his arms hanging down.

Flip started to run. So did I. If we got closer, Elvan could hear. But when he saw us move, he turned away and started running himself, to the other end of the bridge. Flip froze in his tracks and reached out an arm to stop me. Hoping, I guess, Elvan would stop again and see we weren't chasing him.

But there was a sound like a shotgun blast, and I saw rotten floorboards drop into the lake under where Elvan was. For a second, he looked like he was running in place. Then there was another bang, and Elvan dropped through the floor.

We were still on the path. So we could see him fall. He dropped like a sack of grain, but he suddenly stopped. The whole bridge creaked.

At first, I thought he was hanging on there, holding on with his hands. I thought he'd do better to let go and drop down into the water. Even if he couldn't swim, we could. We could save him.

But then, I saw his arms were dangling down by his sides. He was hanging from the floor of the bridge by his neck.

We made a run for the bridge. Without planning it, Flip went to one handrail, and I went to the other one. There were iron strips that ran along under the metal sides. We kept to them and never stepped on the old floorboards. I had to look down to plant my foot at places where the fancy ironwork on the sides didn't get in the way. But I tried not to look back down at the water through the cracks in the floor.

We worked our way along, keeping pretty even with each other. I kept trying to balance my weight, so that if I started to fall, I'd pitch over the railing, straight down into the lake and not back through the floorboards.

By the time we got to the middle point and could see the rest of the bridge sloping off down to the other shore, we saw Elvan's head. It was at a crazy angle, right down level with what was left of the floor.

Still, I didn't understand. Why hadn't he fallen straight through and down? The big part of him had crashed right through.

There were splinters of wood all caved in around him. We were up to him, hanging onto the railings and looking right down into Elvan's face when we saw. Under the flooring right there were two iron beams, crisscrossed to support the floor. He must have lunged to one side as he was falling because his neck wedged into the angle of the iron beams.

Later, that's how they said it must have happened.

Elvan's eyes were open. Like he was looking up in our direction. Only beyond us. He was dead.

"Goddamn us," I said, looking across at Flip. "Oh, goddamn us."

DUNTHORPE MORNING CALL

September 27

LOCAL YOUTH EXPIRES IN FREAK PARK ACCIDENT

Early last evening, Elvan Helligrew, 13, was killed on the condemned footbridge spanning the Marquette Park duck pond. The youth and two of his playmates, all students at the Coolidge Middle School, were in the vicinity of the bridge, which is barricaded by sawhorses owing to the deteriorated condition of the plank floorboards. The Helligrew youth entered upon the bridge and fell through it 28 feet from the southern approach, having run across the longer portion of the span before the fatal fall.

According to Black Hawk County Coroner, V. H. Horvath, death was caused by a broken neck. In his fall, young Helligrew's head wedged in the juncture of two metal supports, directly below the collapsed floor surface. Death was apparently instantaneous. Coroner Horvath has termed the fatality "death by misadventure" and has called further investigation unnecessary.

Dunthorpe Park District officials have not made themselves available for immediate comment.

A lifelong Dunthorpe area resident and a member of the Mount Gilead Methodist Church, Elvan Helligrew was the only son of Mr. and Mrs. Austin L. Helligrew, 62 Old Plymouth Drive, Beechurst Heights. Funeral arrangements are incomplete.

DUNTHORPE MORNING CALL

September 29

LETTERS FROM OUR READERS

Sirs:

I feel certain that I speak as the voice of the entire Dunthorpe community when I point the finger of outrage at the Park District's *criminal* negligence in allowing the deathtrap that spans the Marquette Park duck pond to lure a child at play with his fellows to an untimely grave.

I demand the immediate prosecution of Park District officials who have allowed the tax-supported public parks to degenerate into notorious *wastelands*, the resort of derelicts, and the site of any number of unsound structures that stand as a clear and present danger to us all.

If there are any real men left in this community, I charge them to *rise up in a body* and to raze this deadly bridge and burn the woods around the dreadful duck pond. I speak in the name of the *innocent children* of our once-fine community.

Print this letter in its entirety.

(signed)
(Miss) Bernadette Dunthorpe
Number 1 Dunthorpe Boulevard
Dunthorpe

Richard Peck is the author of more than twenty highly acclaimed novels for young readers, including *A Long Way from Chicago*, a 1999 Newbery Honor Book; *Ghosts I Have Been*, a *New York Times* Outstanding Book of the Year; and *Father Figure*, an ALA Best Book for Young Adults. In 1990, he received the American Library Association's Margaret A. Edwards Award, which honors "an author whose book or books, over a period of time, have been accepted by young adults as an authentic voice that continues to illuminate their experiences and emotions, giving insight into their lives."

Mr. Peck was born in Decatur, Illinois, and attended Exeter University in England, DePauw University, and Southern Illinois University. He lives in New York City.